Ari Wolf has resided in Western Canada all of his life. He is a father of two, stepfather of two, and grandfather of two. He currently lives with his wife Melanie in their peaceful, empty house.

At a young age, Ari discovered the joy of storytelling through the embellishment of some truths, and sometimes dealing with their consequences.

This work is dedicated to the larger than life personalities I've had both the pleasure and pain to share my years with.

Ari Wolf

STANDING

AUSTIN MACAULEY PUBLISHERS™
LONDON • CAMBRIDGE • NEW YORK • SHARJAH

Copyright © Ari Wolf 2023

All rights reserved. No part of this publication may be reproduced, distributed, or transmitted in any form or by any means, including photocopying, recording, or other electronic or mechanical methods, without the prior written permission of the publisher, except in the case of brief quotations embodied in critical reviews and certain other non-commercial uses permitted by copyright law. For permission requests, write to the publisher.

Any person who commits any unauthorized act in relation to this publication may be liable to criminal prosecution and civil claims for damages.

This is a work of fiction. Names, characters, businesses, places, events, locales, and incidents are either the products of the author's imagination or used in a fictitious manner. Any resemblance to actual persons, living or dead, or actual events is purely coincidental.

Ordering Information
Quantity sales: Special discounts are available on quantity purchases by corporations, associations, and others. For details, contact the publisher at the address below.

Publisher's Cataloging-in-Publication data
Wolf, Ari
Standing

ISBN 9781638293286 (Paperback)
ISBN 9781638293293 (ePub e-book)
ISBN 9781638293279 (Audiobook)

Library of Congress Control Number: 2022923560

www.austinmacauley.com/us

First Published 2023
Austin Macauley Publishers LLC
40 Wall Street 33rd Floor, Suite 3302
New York, NY 10005
USA

mail-usa@austinmacauley.com
+1 (646) 5125767

Prologue

State of the Union address, interior of the massive Council Hall of The Americas:

"As the Commander In-Chief of this great council, I come to you tonight with both a grim, yet hopeful message. We have come to the realization that there is a cancer, a very evil cancer lying at the core of everything our founders fought and struggled for – FREEDOM, and PEACE, paid for by the sacrifice of those before us. Yet sadly there are those who rob us of our freedom, who poison our streets, our bodies, our minds, and our children. These people seem to be getting more and more able to harm us, seemingly without consequences. Violence, fear, and suffering have finally come to a head on this great continent, and along with it has come a time for us all to deal with it."

"As of midnight, June 21, 2062, we the government of this continent has committed to you our brothers and sisters, to rid society of the cancer that has held us in its iron grip for so many years. Over the next year, Special Forces in association with all facets of branches of the coalition's Continental Intelligence will initiate an operation solely dedicated to enforcing a new 'Zero Tolerance' mandate. These groups are empowered to physically neutralize those who overstep the laws now common, as outlined over the last two weeks of parliament. Murderers, rapists, pedophiles, thieves, drug dealers, and all other individuals stated within the new legislation that will be formally ratified today, will be identified and terminated immediately. Absolutely no deviance from the mandate will be tolerated. As the Holy Bible states in Genesis:' Whoever sheds the blood of man, by man shall his blood be shed'… God have mercy on our souls." "The thousands in the great hall stood cheering and clapping, and sounded as if the clouds opened and thunder roared out of the heavens.

Chapter 1

Three years later: The five of us followed Sergeant Overton into the light of the subway platform to check our Model CS-422 Articulating Rifle Systems, affectionately known as 'scramblers.' I put my helmet on, felt the air pillows inflate to hug every contour of my skull, and then activated my HUD, immediately the digital display just under my line of vision initialized and set – it still takes a few minutes to adjust to, even after all of this time. I focused on the billboard at the other end of the station, and pulled my scrambler up to my shoulder to set line of sight. Immediately, the faint red crosshairs appeared and centered on the white teeth of the pretty boy model on the advertisement. I felt the familiar squirm of the scrambler's barrel adjusting to the crosshair's path I had chosen – we never miss.

"Ellis!"

"Target 30.2 meters," the headset casually announced in that deep, sultry woman's voice. I quickly placed the crosshairs on the bottom of the garbage can in front of the billboard and instantly, "Target 29.7 meters" Audio matched video, all systems were a go.

"Ellis, get your ass over here!" Overton growled again.

"Sorry Sarge."

"I'm going to say it only once. What we have here is a runner, look up on you screens, it's scrolling up right now. What you have is a recent image taken from the victim's hot spot. This image is about as clear as they could ever come, thanks to the boys at Imaging. We have a Caucasian male, nineteen to twenty-four years of age, approximately one hundred and eighty pounds, black hair, shit-brown eyes, black "T" shirt, and denim coat and pants. He raped and killed a nineteen-year-old girl while she was walking home alone from the university about a kilometer away from here." Looking each of us in the eye, "Target is to be considered potentially armed, so we will approach him with caution. Deviance Squad 17 chased him into the other side of this subway tunnel, and we're going to drop him before Seventeen gets the credit. Is everyone all clear on that? Everyone has all of his headsets engaged and clear to go?" Nodding with us, "Good – let's roll. Ward and I take the point, Sygnarowsky and Hwang take center behind Ward and me, Ellis, you and Jonesy take the point."

We moved about one-hundred yards into the tunnel off of the platform when the light degraded to beyond the shits. "Activate enhance mode on your headsets and acknowledge. I guess when they shut the train down so we could come in here they really shut everything down – Overton activated."

"Ward on."

"Ziggy on."

"Hwang ditto."

"Ellis activated."

"Jones a go."

We still kept rolling down the tunnel, which thanks to the headgear was lit-up and computer enhanced through our visors like the top had been peeled off of the tunnel at noon, less a few stray pixels here and there.

Overton put his hand up to signal a stop and paused himself to listen to the headset. "Yeah, it's me, Smitty – where you be?" Unfortunately, we had the liberty of only listening to our commander and him alone when in-pursuit, as no other transmissions were allowed on our sets. We lived and died as a unit under his command.

"Right, before we get to kilometer marker thirteen, which is supposed to be midway in the tunnel, make sure to call-in so we don't end up shooting your sorry asses…over." We were waved forward again and kept moving along, never breaking a crouched half-run in the stale, dark tunnel. After about five minutes of advancing and covering, Lewis raised his hand to signal us to hold our position. "Engage heat." He whispered into the wire in his helmet as he fell into a crouch. The only thing I saw as Lewis lowered his arm from the hold command, was the heat pattern of the runner backed into a depression in the tunnel wall about five meters ahead of us. The heat trail spreading from all around him made him look like a negative photo of the Shroud of Turin. The little dink was looking right back at us through a massive vintage set of night vision glasses, holding a big revolver lowered at Lewis. The tunnel exploded two shots from the big gun with roars and blinding light that seemed to last an eternity then chased the black tunnel behind us. There were chunks of meat and blood flying off of Lewis in slow motion. He just looked down at his belly and tried pushing everything back in with his shaking, empty hand. He then chuckled and collapsed face down on the tracks!

Ward and I snapped out of it first and fired two or three charges from our squirming guns into the runner, dropping him like a rag doll.

"Jonesey, switch your headset to contact a goddam ambulance NOW!!!" Ward was too charged to take care of feelings as he sprinted to Sergeant Lewis's body, crumpled on the tunnel floor.

"Code 312, Jones, Deev Six, we have an officer down…" Jonesey turned his back away, maybe to concentrate on the coordinates on his screen, probably not.

"Ward to Deev Seventeen, runner down, Sergeant Lewis down…assessing wounds, out!" Turning, "Hwang, what's he got?"

"He's got his fucking guts all over the tunnel and I really don't think he's going to make it…he's barely got vitals!!"

"Put a blood-expander on him, patch the holes and wait for the ambulance to come and take over! Jones, Jones, wake up! What's the E.T.A. of the Medivac?" The strain of being second in command under these circumstances was clearly showing on Ward's face.

"Touch-down is in about eight minutes…" Jones's eyes were glazed over, clearly, he was going into shock at being around this.

Ward, snapping, "All right, you are absolutely fucking useless to me right now. Go to the entrance of the tunnel and make sure they come down the right branch – NOW!!!" Ward stood and shoved Jones into running toward the entrance of the tunnel, but not before throwing a look of pure contempt. "Goddam kids, where the fuck do we find these guys? Ellis, where do we find cute little cream-puffs like you and Jones?"

I had a hard time holding my tongue, actually disgusted that he could joke. "Ward, you were green once too if you don't remember, asshole!" "Yeah, but green and stupid are two completely different things!" Hwang and Ziggy actually both laughed right along!

"Ward, I'm starting to lose him, vitals are going down the shitter in a hurry!" Hwang was clearly scared being in charge of a losing battle.

"Pack him with another expander, he's obviously lost too much blood – get some volume in him!" Ward pushed Hwang aside like a piece of trash and grabbed another bag, pulled the needle cap off with his mouth and moved to put it into a vein himself.

"He's already had two bags, he's bleeding too badly inside, and it's no use…fuck me!!" Hwang and Ward couldn't back pedal fast enough away from Lewis as he sat up in a convulsion, eyes looking around and mouth wide open, then slowly relaxed back – down to die as his last breath left him in a whisper.

Absolute silence, we simply stared at the Sergeant. Ward started laughing maniacally, "Whoa that was fucking creepy!" Still chuckling, "Ellis, mark the time of death for the records into Lewis's headset."

I slowly sank to my knees beside Lewis and bent down to speak my rank number, name, and confirmation of his death that the helmet had already recorded and transmitted back to central. I stood up, shut my helmet down and walked away to gather my thoughts.

Lewis just looked at me through his empty eyes as if he were going to sit up and go boo again.

"Ziggy! Get the fuck over there to the runner and establish his specifics!" Ziggy shot Ward a look as he grudgingly came out from the shadows of the tunnel wall with a cigarette in his mouth, and worked his way to the fallen runner. In the chaos that had transpired within the last three minutes, he managed to slink away and not have to soil his hands at all. Now that the heavy lifting was done, he was okay to take part again. He stepped on the hand of the runner with the gun still in it. Crunching the finger bones under his heel, he twisted his foot and grated his teeth until he was satisfied that the man was truly in "state." Taking off his fanny pack, he threw it to the ground and took one last drag of his cigarette before he knelt at the side of the runner's gun hand, then balanced it on the bridge of the runner's nose. Out of the bag he took a 'BAK' (Body Analysis Kit), opened the sterile blade pack attached, then proceeded to cut the runner's middle finger from its tip to the first knuckle all the way to the bone. He then hooked the lead off of the kit to the end of the same finger, turned the pack on and sat on his heels to wait for the readout.

"Readout coming Ward!"

"What you got," Ward said as he stood-up from his crouched position and looked toward Ziggy.

"The runner's brain is fried save for his motor centers, I guess that means our guns still work the way they should respiration normal, kidneys normal...lungs blah blah blah. The only thing that would have killed this guy was a nasty case of the clapper; as long as we don't donate his dick all will be good. Blood work shows no sign of viral rot."

"Ziggy, contact Good Host or whoever the fuck is on this side of town and tell them we have some transplant information to upload immediately for all of this wet bag. When they come for the runner, tell them to make sure there's enough room in the Medivac to take both the skinner and Lewis. No sense wasting taxpayers' money."

Ziggy rolled the skinner over on his side to check the pockets for cash and immediately let him drop again. "Aw fuck, that really is the smell of death man! Why do the runners always shit themselves, why can't they just pee? I bet if we just used bullets, they wouldn't shit themselves. Fifty years ago they didn't have to deal with this shit, did they? What about the old west and Billy the Kid?" Ziggy stood up pointing to Ward and the rest of us, "He's not remembered for shitting his pants, is he now? What about—"

"What about shut the fuck up and upload the skinner's info so we can get the hell out of here?" Ward said the first words I agreed with since the shift started.

Chapter 2

The Medivac finally came rolling up the tunnel with its whining cell motor, and its mind-numbing lights and siren going full-tilt. It pulled up a few feet away from where Lewis was fallen and the motors entirely shut-down, leaving only the flood and the rotating reds going. Jonesy got out of the back of the ambulance and proceeded to help the attendants bag the Sergeant and load both him and the runner in. In a few minutes, the Medivac was on its way, lights and siren going again to beat all hell in an empty subway tunnel.

"Good thing he had the siren on, all the traffic down here and all." Ziggy did have a way with words.

"Is my brand-new Brownie pack ready to roll out of here? Good! We'll exit the tunnel the same way as in and head home for the night-shift's over." Ward took over control as the senior member unusually well tonight.

Chapter 3

Back at home, finally! I wasted no time in peeling my black squad clothes off and dragged myself into a nice, hot shower. Closing my eyes, I let the recycled hot water beat on my skin, drumming me into relaxation so I could decompress my day. Still shocked that Lewis was gone, I felt like I would see him again at work at the next day. Out of sight, out of mind, it was easier that way.

Then I thought of her, and the scene burned into my brain with her on her back, him on her and she was begging, pleading to me for help. All I could do was run away, and when I finally had the nerve to come back, everything was gone. I softly beat my head against the tiled wall of the shower, not even having the strength to drive the images away. Why did something always take me back there? I tried to force myself to stop sobbing and shut my brain off by beating my head harder! These little bubbles of my past kept floating to the surface and bursting open uncontrollably, as if it were just yesterday. Finally, I forced my brain to close off everything. I got out of the shower and toweled-off, then pulled on what smelled like a fresher pair of boxers than what I had on from the floor.

Slumping down into my couch with a huge sigh and my hands in my hair, I called-up my messages.

"Roger, how come you don't call me anymore? I've left several messages and I swear this will be the last…"

"Skip message." I looked over and saw that pathetic mousy face on the screen, bitching at me as if she were actually still in my life.

"Mr. Ellis, you have just won a fabulous…"

"Skip message."

"Rog…no…I…," I felt as if there were suddenly a thousand unseen eyes looking into my life! My whole body went cold.

"Repeat third message!" This time I watched the video screen.

"Rog…no…I…,"

The image almost looked like an overexposed photograph from about 100 years ago – someone was clearly doctoring the picture on purpose. Picture integrity is impossible to be this bad in this day and age, especially with all of the controls and security in place. "Hold picture and print on my mark. Repeat third message and single frame forward again, again…again…frame back. Good, hold and print." I leaned over to where the picture was printing. I pulled the picture off feed and began looking, almost afraid of what I'd find. These fucking things! High-Tech coming out of our asses, and the picture integrity was still grainy, both on the screen and printouts. It also doesn't help that the caller was calling from a pay phone at night, outside, yet the features could be similar. What the fuck am I thinking! There are about two million people in the city alone that could fit this hazy, grainy outline…but then it hit me! On the top right corner of her forehead, just above her eyebrow was what looked like a scar, just like Alle had from the pop-fly baseball when she was twelve…it's just too fucking impossible! She's dead, and so is that sonofabitch.

Chapter 4

I turned on some overpowering, mind-blowing vintage metal music Sam had dug-up for me, and knelt on the floor of my poor man's Dojo in my bedroom. I bowed my head and began to purge everything I had emotionally. Karate was the one thing that I could do well that I could use to control and shut everything else out. My old man, even with all of the things he did to Alle and me, taught us both well in "Hard-Style." The government trained him extremely well and planted him in several "advisory roles" overseas, and then he passed on his ability and passion he had to fight to us. I worked fluidly for over an hour, knelt and bowed-out of my altar to a picture of my Sensei, Mohammed Ali. Even though he wasn't my master, he's the ideas of a person I respect the most. I refuse to bow to my father. Slowly I rose to my feet, physically and emotionally drained, good. I crawled into the shower once again barely with enough energy to meet the challenge, rinsed-down, toweled off, and then flopped into bed into an instant dreamless sleep.

Chapter 5

"Ellis, what is your fucking problem today? I'm not going to take a man out if he's not in the game." Ward was once again the wonderful motivational speaker.

"Meh." That is the best I could come up with. I still couldn't get over the emotional hangover.

"Well just in case, Ziggy and Hwang are going to be my cover today and you and Jonesey will be your own cover group. A new replacement will be afforded my wonderful guiding hand as of tomorrow morning, and if he is an idiot, you two will have some extra company as cannon-fodder!" Ward laughed.

"Lick my nuts, Ward," Jonesy mumbled under his breath.

"I beg your pardon, Mr. Jones? Just remember to whom you have to answer to Mr. Jones, actually the both of you," looking from me to Jonesey. Poking Jones in the chest, "Now put on your gear and get your asses up to briefing now! I don't want you to make a fool of me on my first day of formally being your superior." Ward had a smug look of satisfaction as he tucked his gloves under his arm and walked out the door to the upper floor with the Ziggy and Hwang.

"If it wasn't for Ward, life would be pleasant killing other people then," Jonesy said to me as we walked down the corridor.

"Hang-tough Jonesy, things always work out the way they need to be," as we walked into the huge, cigarette smoke-filled conference room crawling with men and women from the now twenty-one different Deviance squads. "Where's dick-head sitting?" Looking around the room.

"Ellis, Jones, get your asses over here and sit down!" Ward called and then sat down. We cut our way through the smoke and people and sat under his glare, who now as the acting Sergeant sat at the head of our group in briefing.

"All right ladies and gentlemen, let's begin!" John Wilner, or Black John, had a deep penetrating voice always brought an instant silence to the room. He also commanded respect, in fact total respect wherever he went within the squads because we were his brainchild. Deviance squads were his pride and joy, and everything he knew both mentally and physically we knew, and were forced to as he put it…'Think, improve, and share wherever we go within the system.'

"I'd like to start off with my deepest condolences to Deev Six. The tragic loss of Sergeant Lewis Overton is one that is felt throughout the department for those that worked with him, as well as trained under his command." John looked around the room as if cutting through the smoke. "Effective immediately Leslie Ward is promoted to Sergeant of Deviance Six." Snickers about his first name made the new rank not sound so attractive. Ward's face went beet red. "New business, each Deviance Squad will be enlarged by one person." Soft moans and buzzing instantly filled the room. "All right people, that's enough! These new hands will have been trained directly by the good people in imaging, and will now be put into squads so we can get the freshest picture from the victim. As we all know, time is not a commodity we have a lot of at a scene...any questions or problems?"

"Yeah," Ward said smiling a shit-eating grin, "I hope my unit doesn't get a woman to slow me and my boys down!" Some chuckles came from the group, and you could hear the odd "Asshole" or "Shithead" whispered from the women on the other units.

"Ah yes, Leslie," snickers came again. "Well, don't you worry at all. You and everyone else listen-up, and listen good! These new members are dually qualified: they not only have all of the standard Deev qualifications and training, but they wrote the book on imaging capabilities as well. Ward, you get two new replacements picked just for you and you alone. Effective immediately, you and every other old hand prior to today's graduating class will be trained and certified in imaging by your new additions. Ward, you're going to be trained by a girl," smiling at the now silent Ward who shifted uncomfortably and looked at the floor. "I am not going to let any runners get away because of total reliance on trying to coordinate around the politics of marrying two separate divisions with different goals and different timelines. Ladies and gentlemen as of today we are running as self-sufficient mobile units. Remember, teach learn and share within the system...this message will go to the other units before they go onto their next rotations after you as well. God bless you all. After

Father Leo has blessed you all for the day, head out to transport and be ready to roll when the other units come off shift! All right Father, you may bless these wonderful men and women."

Father Leo, garbed in his finest stepped around 'Black John' and started the daily blessing, which droned on to mostly deaf ears.

Chapter 6

The trip into the basement of the heavily bunkered transport parkade was noisy as hell. All sorts of people were bitching about how they had to learn how to stick probes into dead peoples' brains, or how some 'dork' had better not tell them how to do their jobs or try to change the way they do it. Thankfully, there was also the odd request to 'shut the fuck up.'

We came to our transport to review our assigned area within the city with Deev Twelve coming off shift, looking every bit like a bags of smashed assholes.

"Wolff, was the fishing good last night?" Ward asked casually, lighting a cigarette he took from Wolff's gun belt.

"We got six last night Ward, two dealers in the batch. They were both fucking rotten to the core. We couldn't use any parts out of those guys – aids, rashes, runny noses the whole works," Wolff said laughing at the kills. "Let's see, oh yeah, we had one skinner, two B and E's, and a belt-bomber we got before he pushed the button. They were all good for the donor services at Midtown to part out." Shaking his head like he just finished a good meal, "Man I love my job," spitting on the ground beside the transport.

"Well boys and girls, here comes our new meat and mmm…mamma, it sure looks good," Ward purred as the new recruits were escorted by the shift boss to our transport.

"Sergeant Wolff, this is Private Marion Stoesz. She will be here at you next shift to train you and your crew for imaging, as well as be brought up to speed with her practical field training. Your crew, as well as Ward's is the last to have a female component added to it. Ward, these are Privates Helen Chomyn and Annette Calahoo. By the way Ward, Wilner said these placements are equals and to quote the big man himself, do "not to fuck with them." The escort accentuated by making quotation marks with his fingers.

"Don't worry, they will still respect me in the morning." Ward rubbed his hands together grinning madly.

"Ward, you fucking clown!! All right boys and…girl, it's off home to bed with all of you. Be back in twelve, same place, see ya, Ward, happy hunting." Wolff passed a lazy, bored salute to Ward on his way past and out of the garage.

"Fire up the motor, we have some serious beef here to push with this baby today," Ward said slapping the side of the transport. "Here ladies, let me help you," Ward said grabbing Calahoo's ass from behind with both hands and caressed her into the transport. She shot him back a look that would melt stone, but said nothing. She simply composed herself and her gear, and then sat down on the bench inside with her face now completely red.

"Touch my ass and die Fuckhead," Chomyn said over her shoulder as she started to climb into the transport.

"Ooh, the dark-haired women have such fire," Ward sassed. As he started to reach for her ass just like with Calahoo, quick as a whip Chomyn's leg shot-out behind her and her heel connected beautifully in the center of Ward's chest knocking him ass-over tits onto the ground. Stunned, Ward slowly started moving again ensuring that he was still alive with each joint he moved. As he pulled his legs forward and sat to get-up, he winced in pain and fought everything he had not to scream, but a low groan came out anyways.

"Don't ever fuck with either of us again Sergeant! You think about that every time you breathe tonight, asshole!! Sir." Chomyn sat right next to Calahoo and glared at him while he managed to pull himself into the transport with one arm, while holding his chest.

"All right let's go, we have a shift to pull!" By the way Ward was holding his hand to his chest and wincing, I don't think he was in much shape to do any running tonight.

I instantly liked this girl. Jonesey and I climbed into the transport grinning, and the two women looked-up in time to see the wink I shot them. The quick smiles let me know they were aware they had support here where it was needed.

Closing the door, Ward hit the intercom mounted on the wall of the armored vehicle, "Driver, squad ready for transport." Gingerly easing down into his designated position at the back of the vehicle by the door, Ward closed his eyes still holding his chest. I looked around at everyone's faces lit by the red light which meant we were in transport and to keep quiet, as the walls only blocked our heat pattern from detection in the unmarked transport, not sound. I must have had the same stupid smile on my face when I looked at Ward's goons, as they gave me scowls and the finger – not very nice. I sure had a good feeling about this group as it stood right now.

Chapter 7

The first few days of field training were pretty uneventful with only a few drug related murders here and there. Nothing really exciting came back at us which was actually quite nice, because we all got some imaging time at our own pace. Ward even seemed somewhat open minded to be taught by this girl, although he was still clearly pouting and sore.

"Okay Hwang now one more time, you still need some work. Where do you put the scanner and why?" Calahoo, now nicknamed "Corky" asked as the whole squad squatted around an old homeless drunk who had been beaten to death and was left laying underneath a bridge just off the river.

"Let's see…you roam around both temporal lobes in order to establish the victim's most alive sounds prior to death on the brain," Hwang said more to walk himself through the steps as he held the teacup-sized box with the display screen across the right temple of the man's head. The screen showed some red and orange areas of light that identified light to moderate brain activity, but still in rapid decay, as Hwang still talked himself through the exercise. Slowly, he rolled to a huge white spot, about the size of a dime on the screen, "Bingo!!"

"Good work Hwang, now you get it. You've got the optimum spot now complete the procedure."

Hwang placed the box on the man's head directly over the spot and held it in place, while pushing two trigger buttons simultaneously on either side of the box. A miniscule whirring noise came from the box while the four opposing anchoring screws threaded into the skull to secure the unit in place hands – free. Then the hair on the scalp was automatically removed, and the skin was sterilized. An odd "pop" emitted from the machine as it cut removed and ejected the piece of skull and soft debris through the side vent in the box, then the grand final as millions of tiny crystalline fiber optics were automatically injected into the hot spot and grew into every available live synapses.

"Come on Hwang," Ward Barked impatiently. "It's already been fifteen seconds and you still have another two spots to do!" Hwang attached the lead from the box to the audio input on the scanner he placed on the ground next to the body, then went to the other side and repeated the same step. Finally, he went to the forehead to do the same thing a third and last time allowing access to the visual processors.

"Very good. Now make sure the three leads are fully secured into the processor and let's see what we have." Corky relaxed back onto her heels.

"Jonesy, get your ass over here, you're always fucking around and you never seem to be on the scene! Now!!" Ward was obviously back one hundred percent normal again.

"Image generating and downloading…audio downloading…merging…" Hwang whispered to himself as each sequence finished through the coding on the box.

"You're a bastard Benny," the box's tiny speaker crackled, "You know that money was mine, and how am I supposed to go to…" The explosion that rocked the top of the bridge that we were under, dropped all of us to the ground instantly. Dust and sediment settled peacefully down to the ground around us like snow as I lay across the smelly old corpse, trying to catch the breath that the percussion had knocked out of me.

"Deev Two calling central, large explosion and multiple automatic weapons firing in central block…!"

"Deev Ten, I've got fireworks going-off like the fucking Fourth of July here en-route to the south point of Highland Bridge…!" Oddly enough, Ward kept the frequency open for us tonight in all of our helmets of all things. Every unit in town seemed to be under major fire except us.

"Corky, Ellis, Hwang – stay here to try and get through to base and to keep an eye of things underside while the rest of us go topside to see what the hell is going on! Jonesey, you and Ziggy go up on the east side of the bridge and Chomyn will go up west with me, and make goddam sure your headsets and visors stay activated! Got it??"

"Roger that Ward." I could tell Jonesey was absolutely thrilled with the choice of partners.

"Let's go!!"

My heart was racing – it was about damn time something was going on.

"Ward, this is Jones, we're at the top of the bridge, and…oh my God." The silence that followed scared the hell out of all of us. "Look at this."

Transmitted to our HUD's was the image of the city on fire. Everywhere there were fires, fireballs, explosions, and tracer rounds lighting up the night. The toy-like "pops" and "booms" sounding almost comical, surreal.

The radio started to bring us back to reality, buzzing with confusion and chaos around the city that the other squads are dealing with.

"Jonesey, you and Ziggy will come across to the center of the bridge and down to the blast site. Me and Chomyn will cover your asses! Do you read??" All logged in affirmative, and then the two started slowly up the side of the bridge embankment to the deck, and down the road to the blasted building.

The sound of the alarms from the building confirmed that Central registered the blast, and I finally got through to report. "Deev Six responding to a single explosion at Hawthorne and Twin, request fire assistance!"

The second explosion was even stronger than the first. The screaming over the headset seemed to last forever as the three of us under the bridge scrambled to the top to find Chomyn kneeling over an unconscious Ward, and Ziggy doing chest-compressions on a glass-eyed Jonesey. The fire ball that used to be a building burned fiercely behind them. This simply wasn't happening!

Instantly, a dark green transport came to life twenty meters in front of us, and leapt into motion directly at us with its screaming cell motors and blinding lights. At the last second, the van swerved to readjust and take – out as many in one pass as possible. Chomyn managed to drag Ward's ass out of the way of the speeding cube van by inches, but all Ziggy did was freeze – he just stayed there motionless. "Ziggy, move your ass out of there...Ziggy...Ziggy!!!" I ran to drag both him and

Jonesey out of the path of the van but all I could do was recoil at the last second to save my own ass! I'll never forget the sickening dull thud of Ziggy being hit and flying over the van, Jonesey under, dragged like bits of garbage on the road. He rolled free after a few infinite seconds as the van rounded the corner.

"NNNNOOOOOOOOOOOO fuck!!!!" I couldn't say anything else as I ran to Jonesey, who was now a completely fucked-up mess. There was no way God or technology could fix him, or Ziggy, wherever the fuck his arm went! I looked up as I heard the squealing of tires. The van was taking the turn-out to the small road underneath the bridge where we had found the bum.

Yelling over my shoulder, "Visors down and keep to my frequency, and find out where the fuck support is!" I could catch a clear shot at the van as it came around the turn-out and onto the road on the beltway, providing I could get across the street and down the embankment in time. While I was sprinting across the street, I ripped-open the guard on the holster I keep on my thigh, and pulled-out my favorite piece of history, my father's special – issue pistol. I sure as hell wasn't going to stop this van with our scramblers, as they were only made for hunting animals and electronics, not metal at 100 kilometers per hour. I gave everything I had to clear the guard-rail and get down the embankment to get in position in order get good shot at the motor in the front of the van. All I wanted to do was stop the van. I would worry about its contents afterward.

As the van raced by on the shoulder of the road, oblivious to my presence, I whipped up my visor and shot, seeing the mark open-up on the left side of the van's motor housing. Steam and smoke filled the entire road with the van still racing on by, and I sprinted after it.

The van's engine finally seized and the wheels locked about one hundred meters from me, screeching into a service alleyway between two aging warehouses. The steam and smoke absolutely filled the roadway, engulfing everything around it.

I didn't hear or see any movement around where I assumed the van to be. Regardless, I approached the alleyway hugging one of the factory walls. My breathing was hard to control and thoughts were pretty fluid and barely in-check. I had to come back to focus! Poor Jonesey, twenty – three and just…shit!!! I forgot to put my visor down and enable my helmet!! Pulling it down, immediately…

"Ellis, answer!" Chomyn almost sounded scared.

I crouched with my pistol readied and whispered, "Ellis here, what's the status?" "Ellis, thank Christ you're okay! We have some regular forces and support teams due in ten to twenty."

"That's the best they could do."

"The whole town has gone apeshit! That is the best they could do Ellis."

"I'm going after the van in the alley. The steam has died down enough to move up." Night vision is probably fucking useless in the steam cloud, but it will help with everything around it. I'm going in with heat sensors activated." I put the pistol back into its holster on my thigh and pulled – out my scrambler again.

"I'm behind about thirty meters. I see your ping. I'll keep your bony white ass covered. Hwang, Corky, stay put to direct support to us and coordinate a medical transport for Ward and sweeping crew for Ziggy and Jonesey. With Ward and Ziggy both down and out, Ellis is the acting co now."

"Roger that." The two came through at once on the headset.

The damned steam was finally clearing, so I decided to move before my advantage of cover was taken away completely. I neared the stalled van to look at it, under it, in it – nothing, yet I felt someone close…I raised my scrambler instinctively. "Helmet, engage night vision, overlap heat sensor, starlight…" All of a sudden, the night exploded in a digitally-enhanced light. Everything could be seen clearly enough as in daylight, except the steam still made the picture extremely blurred as the sensors could not build a picture from it because of the mixed heat and cold, and how it changed so fast. I looked at the van again and could see the motor, its hottest parts in brilliant red, blue and yellow, everything else was computer – enhanced to be actual. I looked on the hood of the van, but had to look away in order not to vomit. There, on the front of the grill spreading onto the hood, were little blobs and chunks of dark black against the white-hot hood-pieces of Jonesey and Ziggy that tore away and stuck.

"Ellis, watch your fucking…" the rest was a noisy blur of Chomyn screaming and her scrambler firing to directly behind where I was standing. The perp clubbed me a good one on the head regardless, and dropped me instantly.

I was too busy trying to drag myself to my knees and stay conscious to really care what just happened. The next thing I knew, Chomyn was at my side, pulling the pieces of my helmet off to see what was left underneath, "You lucky sonofabich! I saved your ass! Your head's bleeding, but you're still alive."

I started to open my mouthy in protest, "Fuck you Ellis, besides, I'm the next one up to go with you on your ass, and you have to listen to me!"

The authenticity of what she was saying hit home as all I could do was sit. I threw my scrambler to the ground so I could squeeze my head together with both hands so I could at least speak in a whisper.

"What's that? Ok tough guy. I feel so much better having your beat ass covering me out her in a potentially dangerous situation. You just sit there and drool for a bit." Then she slinked away like a cat before I could try to say anything audible to convince her otherwise.

I finally forced myself to see clearly through a very tight squint, and clawed my way up the van to a crouching position and realized gravity made my head hurt worse. Once everything stopped shaking and wobbling, the pain finally became tolerable enough to go and try to find Chomyn. I gingerly pulled myself up to standing, removed my pistol, and walked as quietly as possible into the alleyway to the left of the stalled van. The steam and smoke hadn't quite thinned out to make things easily seen, but I could kind of see the shadows, if need be. The left side of the wall seemed to offer the best defenses with its dumpsters and piles of trash.

I stepped on something alive that cursed, "You stupid prick, I told you to stay put!"

"I was lonely, is that okay with you?"

"Fuck you, just stay behind me! It's hard enough to do this alone let alone with a gimp with a comical museum piece for a gun coming and scaring the fuck out of me!" The noise up in front of us thankfully shut her up.

"What was that, do you have a reading?"

"No, according to the helmet the alleyway is completely clear." She started to stand-up then all of a sudden, a loud growl from behind us made us turn to see an enormous man lunging toward us full bore with a very wicked curved knife. Before I could get a shot off Chomyn's scrambler had already discharged and stopped the raging hulk in a pile at our feet.

"What the fuck was…" I turned toward Chomyn to see an equally ugly knife coming, that I managed to catch by the wrist inches before it stabbed into her neck. I looked up through the mist to see the face the hand belonged to, and there was an equally ugly man similar to what we had just fallen. The face was older, intelligent, and pockmarked poking through full-body heat insulating suit. No wonder we never saw him through the helmets! His sickly smile, and his dark eyes made my blood chill. In that brief moment that his smile had frozen me, a left palm struck the side of my head and down I went for the second time tonight. I scrambled to get to my feet, but the kick to the ribs slowed that down somewhat. "Shoot him for fuck sakes…" I managed to get out between gasps trying to get my air in my deflated lungs.

"I can't…the helmet is jammed and I can't get a good shot without taking you with it!"

Immediately I was grabbed by the hair and pulled standing into a choke-hold. I could feel the sharp hot breath on my cheek as I started to feel the sweet comfort of unconsciousness coming to save me. "Bye bye sweetheart," was a hoarse, rasp in my ear.

Fuck this!! This guy surely has testicles. The screaming that followed in my ear let me know I had at least one of those boys in my grip. He would have to cut my hand off before I let go. The choke hold instantly loosened enough for two consecutive backward head blows to the bridge of his nose that broke me free completely and almost dropped me as well with the damage done to my head already.

Desperately trying to clear his tearing eyes from the hits, he knew he was vulnerable. I feigned in with a punch to the head, he went to block and I slid to the ground and kicked his feet in to collapse out from under him. He started to fall but caught himself, then went standing again with a slow, calculating smile.

"A real pro we got here. Come on boy, let's go," breathing in controlled rasps. He spat blood and gestured me forward.

A blocked punch from him, and a blocked counter-punch from me over and over. He was matching me move for move, and I was starting to get pissed-off!

I remember when I was about eight clearly, "Come on, Momma's little fag boy can't do it? Your fucking sister can, and you're gonna stay here until you can too! I am your teacher, your god, and you will do as you are told! There is no other option! Now again, reset and stop your goddam crying and do it right!" The stinging slap from my father brought home the fact that it wasn't perfect, again. This would keep coming until he saw it perfect, or fit to do otherwise. Alle sat in the corner watching, completely emotionless. When he concentrated on me, she was safe from the drunken master, monster. The move came back to me like a familiar friend taunting me.

I went in through his guard with an outside punch to disorient him, kicked his left knee in backward to drop him to his knees, and then rolled around to his back with an open palmed punch to the back of the head, then elbow to the kidneys to flatten him onto the ground, "fucking shoot him now, Chomyn!!"

She let a charge go unassisted by the helmet. The whole body did the familiar spasms, and then ceased entirely. "Christ Ellis, where did you learn that shit?" Chomyn asked as she walked toward me. She pulled the retractable microphone string out of the helmet to tell Hwang and Corky to send support, and sill clearly dazed went to the man she had just fallen. I didn't even have time to warn her, the man rolled over from his stomach to grab her leg and bring her to the ground. All it took was one punch in the face for her letting out a pathetic, sickening squeak. She fell back to the ground in a lifeless pile, blood trickling from her nose and freshly split upper lip. I was grateful she stayed unconscious.

He looked up from Chomyn and slowly smiled that sickly smile, to reveal a tiny black mouthpiece with a flashing red light on it. He slowly pulled himself standing onto his good leg, and then spat the smoking mouthpiece onto Chomyn without taking his eyes from me, "gotta love the miracle of technology."

Instinctively, my anger pulled me in to strike this man. I focused everything I had on the one punch, and he didn't even move, he just stood there and smiled that fucking smile!

"Rog."

No way, there was absolutely no way I could be hearing that voice. That voice was long gone, buried. It sent chills down my spine and froze me where I stood. My hands slowly fell to my sides. "Alle, but…"

"I know." The smoke from the van, and the night hid her from me. All I could see was her outline I knew couldn't be there, "be a good boy and keep your head down Rog." The roundhouse kick she delivered lifted me off-of the ground and flat onto my back. Sweet darkness.

Chapter 8

My mother's funeral, I was too young to understand what was going on. Dad, I distinctly remember, seemed almost bored with what was going on with the ceremony to the point of being annoyed. Alle stood beside me in the rain holding my hand, crying like there was going to be no end in sight.

Chapter 9

"Your fucking coward mother's dead! The stupid bitch shot herself in the head," Dad screamed wearing his best grimy T-shirt as he pulled his fingers to his head like a gun. "She's left me to hang here and feel sorry for her – fuck her, and fuck you if you're stupid enough to fall for it!" I saw Alle run past the crack in my door into her room crying. Her door slammed. From the kitchen, pouring himself a drink, "you're just like your fucking mother. No guts, just run away!!"

Chapter 10

I heard Alle crying, it had been so long since I had heard that. "No Dad, get the hell out of my room!!"

"You mouthy little bitch," I heard our father's drunken voice scream out slurring, then a slap and Alle crying again. "This is all you mother's fault!" Alle's bedroom door slammed, now with both voices contained in her room, then all I heard was the low rumblings of my father's voice. I couldn't make out what they were saying, but the way she kept sobbing, I knew it was bad. All I could do was wrap my head with my pillow in bed so I didn't hear what was going on. I convinced myself it wasn't what it was.

Chapter 11

Years passed. "Come on Honey, Daddy knows you can do it. Try on more kick with your little brother." I took offense to being called that. My size, for a fifteen-year-old, was small but over the past couple of years I learned more than enough from Sensai Dickhead, but Alle still towered over me both in skill and size to make up for it.

"Fuck you, and fuck your Honey shit!" Absolute hatred now, along with the emptiness behind those eyes.

"Fuck me huh!! Tough bitch now?" instantly his demeanor switched to monster. His surprise roundhouse kick to her head was easily blocked by Alle. She dropped to her knees and the flat palm to his groin dropped him like a rock. All I could do was stand there and look in absolute shock and fear with my jaw hanging open as he rolled onto his belly to try to catch his breath. What was she doing? What was she going to do once he was standing again? I frantically looked for a place for us to run.

The next thing I knew she was down, bleeding from the split in her lip and clawing at her throat with her eyes bulging, trying to recover from the consecutive punches landed on both. He bent down and grabbed her by her hair and dragged her off to her bedroom.

"I see Daddy's gonna have to teach your sister some manners! Get out boy, and don't come back for a while."

Alle was crying out loud now. "No, Roger stop him, please! Oh God no stop it…!" I didn't know what to do, I curled up into a ball in the corner and sobbed. If I stopped him, it would be me.

I broke from the room running. I had to get away from there as quickly as possible! Out the front door and into the street I flew into the flood of the night. I ran, and ran, and ran to the point where I finally was so exhausted, I could not feel anymore. Finally, I hid pushed as far into the edge where steel meets cement in the underside of a noisy overpass. My world had completely unraveled.

Chapter 12

The sun was just starting to paint the east sky red. I had fallen asleep, the rain had stopped, but the chill was horrible. I forced myself to stretch from the cold ball I had been in and convinced myself I would warm-up walking. I staggered toward home, eyes red and my sleepless body numb and slow. Even wrapping my arms around myself didn't help to relieve the chill in my bones. I wasn't convinced it was from the weather anyways.

A police car went roaring by with the bells and whistles going to beat all hell. I barely even noticed. A fire engine went by, same thing. A couple more sirens bore down a few miles behind me, coming closer and closer and finally went right by me on the street while I walked on. Another siren came up and passed me, and then it finally sunk in to look up in the direction I was going. Slowly, there was a sickly black smudge rolling into the morning sky where I was trying to go – home!! My fatigue dropped away and my feet came to life. I ran as fast as I could toward my home, my sister.

I got as far as the line of police and fire vehicles only to get held back by an officer who screamed and shook me to attention while I frantically tried to claw past him. I looked slowly around his barrel chest and that's when everything went into slow – motion, sounds turning only to a murmur. The house, and the one beside it, were enveloped in a total firestorm! Firemen and equipment fought to try to find a way inside. In the end, all they could do was try to cool the fire down and protect the other houses around it. The policeman's firm hold became an embrace as my legs failed me and I sobbed like a baby into his chest.

Chapter 13

Days later, there was simply nothing left in the smoldering ruins but some old charred beams from the house, some metal bits and pieces from the furniture's heat-warped springs, and the cement foundation. I walked through the ruins as if it were a dream. This could not be my house, there's not anything familiar here. There was something that looked like the fireplace where Mom rocked me when I split my lip when I was six, crying with me, but that is a fading dream too, a hundred years ago it seems.

"I'm sorry about your losses, son. Your father's and sister's remains were taken to the medical examiner and identified today. I wish there was something I could do to help." He stood there like I was to say something profound, but I just turned and ran away, just kept going. "Son, son, come back – we have people that can help you. Son!"

"Jesus Burjour, just let the boy go for a bit. He'll be back in an hour or so." The detective's partner interrupted.

Chapter 14

Three years later: The rain seemed to come down in a solid sheet for two straight days, and into tonight. I crouched under my makeshift lean-to in the alleyway behind the strip mall in Hugh's Corner off of the open-air market, and my waxed cardboard blankets seemed to be tiring of the rain as quickly as I was. I had grown accustomed to the cold and being hungry, and alone, but I liked it. It was just me to worry about, keeping with the safe bums and junkies that shared the city of cardboard and other random shit in the alley with me.

I had just drifted-off and was started by the sounds of a girl screaming up the oddly vacant alley. Her cries for help make me cower at first as reflex, but then I forced myself to venture out of the protection of my shelter to see what was going on. Cautiously, I rolled-out onto the cement, stood up and then pulled the tarp back down behind me.

"Help me…oh God no mmmph," her cry was muffled as one of the two dark shadows tearing at her clothes covered her mouth.

"Ow, the stupid bitch bit me!! Hold her down already!!" Three consecutive dull thuds and smaller cries told me she was unconscious or damn near, I prayed she was almost out.

Crying, "Please, someone help me," Sobbing ever so faint.

In the shadows, the tearing at her clothes continued even at more of a frenzied pace now. I couldn't handle this again. I ran down to the end of the alleyway near the chain – link fence, and came upon them full tilt. One of the men had his knees on her hands feeling her breasts from under her shirt, which he then pulled up around her neck and cat called. The other piece of shit was already inside her! And the girl, the poor girl wasn't even unconscious, she just stared up at the sky with blank eyes, bloody nose and her lip split and bleeding, rocking with each thrust of the sickening man.

As I approached at full speed, I landed a front kick right to the underside of the balls of the man inside her. The scream that came from the man was more than gratifying, as well as relieving seeing as I was assured, he would be out of the way for a couple of minutes.

The next man didn't even have a chance to pull his hands off of her breasts and stand to defend himself before I carried around and kicked his front teeth into his mouth. He fell right off of her onto his back, thrashing around clutching his now bloody face screaming murder. I jumped onto his chest and began hitting him with straight-palm punches to the face and head over and over until he stopped moving.

"You sonofabich, you're gonna fucking die!" A strong, putrid arm wrapped itself around my neck and lifted me to my feet. I was dragged backward, deliberately kept off-balance to one of the brick walls on the building in the alleyway, and my face forced up and down the walls like a goddam cheese grater! The first few times hurt like hell, and regardless of my struggle I couldn't break free!! "Now you little piss-ant, you're gonna meet your maker!" He was hoarse and out of breath. I thought I could use that to my advantage, but the grip got even tighter. Now I was in some serious trouble, I started to black-out. Just as I was pulled away from the wall to take a really good run at it with my head, I had my last chance. The wall came rushing toward my face and I used my forward momentum to plant my feet on the wall and run up and over, throwing my body over his head and out of his grip. Now I had the advantage! I was behind him and he had no idea what had happened.

I grabbed him from behind and buried my fingers into his eyes until something like soft grapes gave in the sockets. Still hanging on, I gave him knee hits to the kidneys over and over again, then his spine. As I pulled his head back, I couldn't control myself. I just kept hitting, my screams overpowering his. Then I felt the snap of his spine and heard the piss hit the pavement through his pants. His body started to spasm, then sagged lifeless to the ground. I helped him on his way by giving a quick twist to his neck to hear the second snap. Now it was done. Falling to the ground on my hands and knees, I gasped for air and struggled to come back down.

I wiped the blood off of my face with my sleeve and looked around the alleyway to find the girl huddled in-between a dumpster and the outside wall of a building, shaking, constantly pulling her dress down to hide more of her body than that dress possibly could even before it was ripped. I inched toward her, "Hey, it's all done, it's over with. They won't bother you anymore. Now come on out…I'm not going to hurt you…there we go." I gave my best smiley-face and motioned her closer. Slowly, like some scared puppy she came out. Her scared eyes were going everywhere as she kept pulling at her dress, sobbing quietly. "I'm Roger, Roger Ellis, what's your name?" I don't even know if she knew I was there behind those poor, dead eyes.

Chapter 15

She never said a word in those eight months we were together, no complaints, no tears, nothing. I was just so happy to be needed by someone. Someone was relying on me to get food and shelter for us-I had a purpose, I made this better. I talked to her day-in and day-out and constantly she led me by the hand to take her to the bathroom, to eat, to bathe, never able to be alone. And then one day her hand just dropped from mine, stopped dead in her tracks as if someone had taken her batteries out. All she would do was sit there, or lie there. Near the end she would sometimes miss going-out to the bathroom.

The day finally came when the baby she carried from the night I met her started to arrive. I had made such a nice lean-to in a wooded as far off of the bay area as practical, as I had it in my head the sea air would be so good for both her and the baby. The baby, even for my first time delivering, and having no idea how a woman, girl, was wired down-south went reasonably well-thank God for the book mobile. She never even made a peep through the whole thing. He was gorgeous; I named him Gabriel. I could tell by the way she said nothing or even looked at us that she approved.

I cleaned the baby and mother as best as I could and tucked him under her arm to feed and sleep beneath the false floor, I had dug to hide them. While they rested, I went off to find us some food for my family.

When I got back a couple of hours later, I saw the girl was sitting in a lawn chair just under the brim of the lean-to she looked so pale, and so peaceful smiling looking out over the bay! "It's nice to see you moving on your own finally I…" I saw the blood soaking through the comforter she had around her, and pulled it back! I sobbed for most of the night with the hungry baby crying on my knee. She had sliced herself with an old filet knife I had stashed for our protection, from her crotch to her ribs, and across again. The pain of what had happened was too much for her to endure.

Chapter 16

A little time had passed and I had gotten myself a shitty job washing dishes in a shitty little lunchbox where the freaks and the assholes coming off of a high or big party at the local bars would hang out. If it wasn't for the regular beat cops coming in for coffee and warmth, the place would have been tits-up years ago. One day, I looked-up from the dishes to see a vaguely familiar face. "Ellis, how the hell are you doing? It's been a few years now. How's things been going?"

"All right, I guess. Keeping busy now that I have a mouth to feed," I said, looking up from the sink.

"A mouth to feed? Boy, you sure got your plate full now huh?"

"Yeah, and it's about all I can do to keep things even."

"I hear you. And the mother?"

"It's just me and Gabriel. There's no 'other.'"

"I'm sorry to hear that…hey Ellis, I'll be honest with you, I have been keeping an eye out for you. When your father and sister passed away, I was in charge of your case, and well, I looked into your family history and you really had a shitty hand dealt to you!"

"Thanks for the memories, Sergeant…"

"Captain. It's Captain now actually, Captain Adam Burjour." He held his hand for me to shake for some time until he awkwardly pulled it back realizing I wasn't about to take it. "Now before you cut me off again, I would like you to listen to what I have to say. I looked into your family history and found your father was a real hardass in the Special Forces, top-notch spook, dean's list, trainer and all. I want to know if you have any of those goodies son."

I was really starting to get pissed-off with this guy, and I guess he got the message when I slammed the tub of dirty dishes, I had been collecting down onto the table in front of him. "I don't see what this has to do with me. Look, just tell me what you want or leave, I have lots of work to do."

"Relax boy." He took a deep breath, looked around and composed. "From the first minute I met you, there was something I liked about you. Others feel you're just another dickhead loser, but I feel I am a pretty good judge of character. I might have a job for you if you want it, or are you a dickhead loser."

"I'm not interested in your fucking job! Look at me, who the fuck is going to hire this!" Screaming now, I raised my arms to reveal more of myself.

"Listen, did your dad teach you any of his fancy-ass fighting shit or not?"

"Yeah," I said sullenly. "It was his life. Our life."

"Was your sister any good with that shit?"

"She made me look like an amateur."

"Good. I'm going out on a limb for this, and I'm going to possibly pay for it. I want your ass to apply to a new unit outside of the police force. Go to Central Headquarters and see Officer Mayer this Tuesday," Handing me a card. "Give this to her and she will help you along the application process and other bull-shit…"

"Why the hell are you looking out for me anyways?"

"Well, part of it is looking good if you are one-tenth as good as I think you are, and the other is I like you. I feel this new unit could help you, and you it." Looking at the clock on the wall then double-checking his watch, "Shit, I gotta go! Look at the time. Don't let your baby or yourself down Ellis. Show up-you're going nowhere here." His words echoed painfully.

Later that night after my shift, I picked up Gabriel from the Cuban lady who looked after him on the floor below me. Walking home with him in my arms, looking at him, feeling him, the answer couldn't have been clearer.

Chapter 17

"Gabriel, where the hell is Gabriel!" I bolted out of bed totally disoriented and dizzy as hell. What was I doing in a hospital bed, inside hospital walls, and hooked-up to wires and tubes! A loosely female bull-nurse came rushing into the room and was already pushing me back in the bed. I started to resist and interject my opinion

"Mr. Ellis, you just can't sit up and expect to walk out of here!"

"Listen to her, Roger. You've been out for a couple of days and before you even think about moving, I think you better get your feet back." The familiar voice boomed.

"Fuck you, Burjour! I still think you're dark enough to be one of those goddam Arabs!"

"His mouth is working fine now nurse; can he go home now?"

"Don't you worry, captain, his feet should catch up to his mouth in about a week or so."

"A week! Fuck that! What time is it? Who's got Gabriel, I've got to get Gabriel!" I stood up to bolt for the door but all I got was a really good view of the floor and some pretty colors bouncing around in my head from the face-plant. I guess I really wasn't quite ready for leaving the confines of my cozy bed with its nice safe railings. The pain was very sobering. "Adam, I think I need to be in here for a week or so." Blood now pouring from my nose in steady stream all over the front of my nice open-assed hospital linens, ass out, I was lifted and dropped leaning onto the side of the bed.

"Here's a wet cloth," the nurse said. "Start cleaning yourself up a bit, I've got rounds to make on less stupid people." And then my angel of mercy left.

"Ellis, you fight your healing time and all you'll end up doing is doubling it! Besides, Emma's got Gabriel at the cottage, and he doesn't even remember you exist, all right?"

"All right," I slowly lowered my naked ass to the bed, my head and bloody nose now pounding violently in unison. "Now tell me what the hell is going on, and what happened to me!"

"The real numbers say that with the creation and evolution of our squads, crime has been cut exponentially, particularly in organized crime with murders, black market, and drug trade. That really eats at the families' money being made. Basically what we have here is an all-out guerilla war with the mafia. They have taken some of their best people, and a shit-load of contracted people, and trained them in counter-Deviance Squad tactics; therefore, you and yours my dear boy are now living targets. Once we pry you away from here, you guys will really have to watch your backs. Do you hear me? Ellis! Ellis!"

"I can't believe it was her, she really is alive but how?" I had sat-up and swung my feet down over the side of the bed, oblivious to the fact that I had already tried this and failed.

"Ellis, weren't you listening to me. We have some serious shit to deal with here…what? Who the hell are you talking about?"

"Alle, it was her. It was definitely her," I said tenderly rubbing the side of my head then looking at my fingers thinking there should be blood there with the way that it felt.

"Enough of that shit Ellis, she's dead! You, me, and this state know it and have certified it! Now come on and get back into bed. The last thing I need for you is to go bonkers on me. Come on, feet in too." He bent to help lift my feet and slide them under the covers.

Chapter 18

"Chomyn, how the hell are you?" Turning her head toward me I really saw her, "Whoa! Wholly shit you look awful!" All around her eyes had started yellowing from the bruising.

"Thanks sweetie, you sure got your color back in a big hurry didn't you ninja Bob?"

Calahoo looked at her, somewhat confused with what she was talking about.

"Don't worry honey, I'm sure you'll see sooner or later."

"Grab a seat gentlemen and ladies, we have a meeting to start." The meeting room was clearly swollen to beyond its intended capacity. Around the smokey room were some familiar faces and a lot of unfamiliar faces. New staff! "All right now, enough and sit!" Black John's powerful voice boomed and captured the room killing all noise except for the odd cough and 'shush.' "Thank you. Now, first of all I would like to give my condolences to anyone who suffered losses in their squad during last week's uprising. Loss is never an easy thing to overcome. Those of you who feel you need it, counseling is available twenty-four, seven. Secondly my dear hangman, the shit has hit the fan." Looking at each and every one of us, "the mafia lords, and all of their big businesses that we have yet to eliminate, effectively have combined their forces in order to break the backbone of our units, and claim back their territory. Third, some of the people that are not here right now were killed in the line of duty, and the others donated organs to society because of their involvements with the very body we are going to be at war with right now. Does everybody understand me?" Everyone I looked at turned pale when they realized there were a decent number of people they were close to missing, and for which reason?

Looking at the girls I mouthed, "Wholly shit! Ward and Hwang!"

"Good, and in our next little gathering you will probably notice a few more seats available on top of that. All I can say is the cancer in these squads is being dealt with!" I could feel the tension in the room mounting. Anybody who had their eyes on Wilner at the podium was a moron. I was too intimidated to even look up, and I hadn't done anything wrong. "Number four, all deviance squads will be reduced to smaller four member units in order to be more effective, mobile, proactive, and less cumbersome while at the same time giving us more squads for coverage. You will go out on foot and will assume the role of hunter squads instead of the reaction or elimination forces we have been to date. Targets will be assigned at the beginning of each shift by an appointed shift captain to your individual groups to keep personnel and assigned targets random. Fifth item on the list, as of today we all are live and on line for information from CIA and FBI." The whole room was dead silent. John Wilner scanned the room for some sort of response that everyone really absorbed what he just said. "I can tell by your stupid looks on your faces that everyone is fine with this so far. Good. Last is a personal favorite of mine-with the access of the CIA's and FBI's information net we also get some of their geeks, as you see scattered about the room cleverly dressed for undercover work. Stand-up and introduce yourselves."

Several men and women stood-up to sheepishly wave and look around wearing their CIA or FBI coats and T-shirts! The laughter broke open the whole room.

"All right, all right enough! Show some pity on these poor souls. We have also addressed the fact that forces are still needed for the 'smaller profile' occurrences that our groups used to look after. Regular forces will assume these responsibilities in strictly an elimination role with back-up from us as needed. All runners from this day on until we can get a feel for what we're up against will be simply eliminated, not evaluated and parted out. People will have to wait for their parts, and will be informed of such soonest. This is going to get a whole lot worse before it gets any better. All right, everyone good so far? Right, now downstairs to the gardens to see your rosters and meet your new partners and teams. Then at 1300 hours, to warehousing to see a display of the new software we're going to add to your headgear, and some of the new hardware some of you will carry. Okay, meeting is adjourned, God have mercy on our souls."

Slowly, everyone got up, and soon was back to the noisy chaos that it was prior to the meeting. "Ellis, I hear from my daughter that you're a real bad-ass with that Karate shit," John boomed as he walked up to me and slammed his huge hand on my back.

"Excuse me sir." Shocked, I had no idea who the hell he was talking about.

"My daughter, Helen. She's given her mother and me twenty-six years of joy, and about twenty-five years' grief." Wilner's laughing seemed almost unnatural!

"You're Wilner's daughter?"

"I took my mother's maiden name, Black John and I figured I wouldn't have a hope in hell of surviving here otherwise."

"She insisted on entering like this, got her mother's fire this one." Smiling with complete adoration as he looked at his daughter. "Anyways, keep it low profile for me Ellis. Calahoo good to see you," she simply nodded, her mouth full of a doughnut, and another in her hand. "Ward and Hwang will not be returning to duty. A few people are pissing through their own dicks instead of a machine because of those two, and I'm really sorry. Bye honey, I have to bolt, got to explain the recent modifications to the regional council and body," quickly bending to give a small kiss on her forehead. "Ellis, you watch out for my girl now that you're running Six. She's all I have since her mother passed away."

Chapter 19

"Harry Schlanker F.B.I., pleased to meet you." His handshake was like shaking a warm, dead fish.

"Roger Ellis, Helen Chomyn, Annette Calahoo," I said pointing to my two partners and myself.

"Nice to meet you all, I hope to have a really healthy working relationship with the three of you." This man was trying way too hard.

"Harry?" I asked.

"Yes."

"Harry, what the hell kind of name is Harry Schlanker? It sounds weird, like some sort of body part, kind of like the piece of skin between your nuts and your asshole." Snickers and a spitting laugh was all the girls could come up with.

"Well it's a European name coming from nobility from the region of…"

"No," I cut him off. He was starting to bore me. "Harry will not do, it leaves too much room for abuse from the other units, and I don't like that shit because that's our right." I was using every bit of will-power to keep myself from laughing. "Let's see, how old are you?"

"Twenty-six, sir."

"No need to sir me, my dad was a sir and he's a dead asshole. Now, twenty-six, glasses, balding." By the way he was feeling the top of his head that was the first time he had ever been told he was thin up-top. "Nothing, I can't think of anything. Hey, do you have any unusual qualities other than your looks?"

At first, he was a little ticked-off at my remarks. "Actually I have quite a reputation with the girls for having quite a large…penis."

"The reputation…hey girls, Harry has a big dick, we'll call him snake!" The poor man.

"Hello Snake!" The sound of those words coming from the two or three hundred voices in the courtyard made the name as good as him being born with it.

Harry came out of there with three phone numbers, one a guy.

Chapter 20

Two of us were qualified to carry the new recoilless-rifle issued to the squads. It was designed for long distance sniper hits from up to four miles with pinpoint accuracy assisted by the headset and multi-staged smart bullets that were shaped like soup cans with both ends cut out of them. Internal fins adjusted continuously on the inside diameter to manipulate flight. The scope interfaced with the bullet to compensate for cross-winds, humidity, temperature changes, and earth's rotation. Any recoil from the series of electro magnets used to propel the projectiles was transferred to its odd-ball hydraulic system that spread it downward across the back of the carrier across its crisscrossed rigid harness. With the laser upgrade, we could also get sound coming back from the target so we could literally get the voices transmitted from the hits as needed without extra equipment over most practical distances. The best part was these guns could be adjusted and used for firing and lodging transmitters, small personnel clearing, and light armor piercing weapons. Calahoo and I were ecstatic that we were the qualified carriers due to the fact that if the technology failed, we still were very competent with the rifle and scope alone in a manual application, and were assured the highest level of success. Chomyn was a little pissed off that we were the best shots with the things, but she soon got over it once she saw us having to run with the 15 extra pounds strapped to our backs, then it was funny.

All in all I have to admit that in the next two months of training, Snake proved to be a valuable addition. He turned out to be a genius with numbers and computers like working out a few of the bugs in the uplink with the FBI and the CIA's computer systems and our system in order to get them all talking the same language in real time.

The icing on the cake was when he even managed to delete my security clearance when I stepped over the line teasing him one time. The security footage that keeps popping up still shows my total horror clearly as I was taken-down by security in force after I tried logging into the facility with a suspect eye print, alarms and all.

I established Snake a subtle force to be in the good books with.

The one thing that amazed me and the girls all to hell was Snake and his statistics.

"You have twenty-one people within one meter of the target at this point in time. All mobile, circling the target and covering him leaving open spots at an irregular rate as they bump through the crowd. You have about an eighty-six percent chance of taking out one of the bodyguards circling around him before the actual target, and a six percent chance of having the bullet deflect off of a bone inside the guard and missing or only wounding the target."

"You have a one-hundred percent chance of getting my foot in your balls! I personally think you make all of this shit up as you go along!" Calahoo had gotten awfully vocal ever since she had started carrying a big gun.

"You like that gun because it makes you the man you never had. Besides, numbers are the one thing we can count on being stable, unlike women."

"Geek, this is the man you'll never be," Calahoo laughed as she shook the barrel in his face.

"Well, I think we have the makings of a bet here ladies and gentleman. What will the stakes be?" I asked looking at the other three for takers.

"Let's keep it simple," Calahoo said, "because otherwise, people tend to get stupid." Pointing between Snake and me.

"All right, we'll call it dinner. Whoever wins this one has a free meal at the other gender's expense, okay?"

"Done, now shut-up while I set-up." Calahoo attached the disposable mounting leg to the front of the gun, placed in the charge and pushed down on the top of the barrel and heard the now familiar hammer of the leg being shot secure with a charge into the building's ledge.

"Okay gang, time is zero two thirty and the hit should be coming into visual. Helmets on and engaged." I pulled down my visor and felt the helmet's pillows filling with air and hugging my head. "Deev Twelve to Deev Six come in," the helmet headset instantly rattled. "Deev Six activated, do you have visual of hit?"

"Negative. Will advise."

Chomyn turned and whispered to me, "Ellis, shouldn't you mount your gun for back-up for Calahoo, I mean, what if she misses?"

"If she misses, Twelve will take the target like they're supposed to. Two shots or three, won't make a difference on this one." Calahoo was already laying spread eagle on the building's gravel roof with her sights on the nightclub's doorway, with Snake and Chomyn beside her on their bellies spotting with the aid of their helmets. I sat, back against a ventilation duct.

I lifted my gun to the door of the nightclub and instantly the faint crosshairs appeared, "Target 396.3 meters." Stirring me. "Magnify twenty times, stabilize." I said into the microphone wire mounted around the right side of my jaw. Instantly the digitally generated doorway of the club lunged at me and my head went back in a reflex action. "Activate city night vision ten percent." The night was quite clear and the street lights gave off enough light to do the job with the naked eye, but not enough to burn the empty black shadows away in the features of the night that could trick your eyes when it came to judging distances like this. The shadows melted away rather nicely for the contest. I dropped my gun back to a resting position with the muzzle nested on my thigh, "Helmets on, engaged." Three 'rogers' cleared us to go.

"Deev Twelve to Six, target's station is on number five on the set; get ready to roll."

"Roger that. Helmet, station five for audio, transmit for short range." Short range allowed the rest of the unit to hear within one meter of each other during these hits what was being said by the target coming back over the laser.

"Established lines secured, transmitting one meter."

Coming over the spotter's laser, "...the car, I'm ready to go. C'mon c'mon, let's get it moving, I've got things to do and people to see!" An excitable voice came over the station, "Darby, get your ass to the front door, now! Pull up as tight as you can to cover us."

"Roger that." Squealing tires and the hiss of cell motors gave us the signal to ready ourselves. In less than fifteen seconds, five Ambassador – class transports came burning around the corner and screeched to a halt in single file. "We're landed Gene, let 'er rip." Suddenly the club doors flew open and out came a small crowd of people moving like satellites covering the man in the middle. They all circled in order to cover him from any potential harm from any angle, about ten or so bodies beating and pushing anyone within arm's reach in order to clear a path to the car.

"I don't know what the fuck is gonna go down, all I know is we were told to beef up due to a new threat of a hit."

The two shots Calahoo took a split second from each other were absolute pieces of art. The first bullet liquefied the head of the bodyguard in front of the target, then the second bullet, a split second behind, took the target's head off where the bodyguard's head had been. Both shots sprayed the rest of the bodyguards and crowd, driving them into absolute chaos. They scrambled into the center to cover their client and then lift what was left into the car, leaving an obnoxious blood train. Another three rushed to the hit to help the fallen bodyguard before they realized there wasn't much left to guard anymore.

One of the guards kneeling at the side of the fallen bodyguard waving frantically, Everyone get in the cars, oh my god!! C'mon, let's fucking move!! Shit shit, they took out Jinx. Let's fucking move Darby!" In a quick staccato,

"Go go go! Jinx's gone man, step on it!" All five cars sped off in the same direction, doors open on some, legs and arms barely in others.

"Deev Twelve to Twenty-Two, do you have position?"

"Deev Twenty-Two roger that."

Until now, I didn't even know the other two squads were in waiting. This must have been one hell of a target to have had another rifle aimed in and waiting.

"Holy shit boy and girls, I think you might want to see the fireworks with your own eyes, disengage visor." The visor instantly retracted and I stepped right onto the edge of the building like a kid at the zoo looking into the bear pit. From our vantage point on the building rooftop over three hundred meters from the hit, we could easily see the arteries of streets going in every direction, and the target's cars leaving the party.

"Front two transports to Deev Twelve, back three to Twenty-Two. Seven and One to go backup to cover in case of potential error."

"Twenty-Two, roger that." Calm over the air waves.

"Seven, roger that."

"One, roger that."

The two front cars had just turned the corner off the street from the hit, with the last three about six meters away from cresting the corner when five launch trails came from all of our positions. It happened so fast no one knew what hit them or where it came from. The cars were instantly annihilated, contents and all!

"Holy fuck!!" That was the first time I ever heard Snake swear. I looked at the two girls and their blank expressions.

"Nice shooting Calahoo, I think Snake owes you dinner." I had to get the argument started for the ride back.

"Deev Twelve to Six, how many bodies should there be including the hit?"

"Thirteen heads."

"Good hunting Six and Twenty-Two, hope we can all play again."

"Deev Twelve to central, thirteen bodies confirmed to clean up in hit area three, five cars full of crispy critters and two bodies in front of Pip's nightclub. Dispatch fire crews and clean up to assist. Out."

"Central to Twelve, roger that. E.T.A. in about three minutes." You could already hear the sirens wailing off in the distance.

We packed up and went down to wait for our transport, and we listened to central the whole time, even on the ride back for debriefing. A total of twenty-three hits were reported in city wide for the night, with a grand total of thirty-three units performing in them. We all got away with no injuries or deaths. We caught them by surprise. This time.

Chapter 21

"All right boys and girls, let's be getting on with it! Take your seats and shut your mouths!" Wilner's booming voice did very little to ease the buzz and commotion that went on in the room. Voices all over the room were bragging, arms flying in the air showing action and it was all going on all at once. "Now!" Wilner's voice burst like a bomb, scattering everyone to their chairs. "Thank you!" Dead silence and no one was moving as Wilner's eyes cut through each and every one of us in the briefing hall. "Now, as I was saying, we all did very well tonight but it was far from perfect, and it is far from over. As it was, two key targets slipped through our fingers. We took out a big chunk of the support network with our hits, but we still have work to do. These assholes will have gone underground so deep they won't even open the door for the good man himself," pointing up. "It will take timing and a whole shit load of skill on our behalf to pull off the rest of the heads off of Cerberus…do I make myself clear?" Looking around the room. "Good, as well as the previous mentioned, you may or may not notice two more people missing from the ranks of our group. One target and three of his support staff were misses because of the blatant involvement of these absent individuals, but their graciously donated organs are serving the others that were in need, and deemed more worthy. With the smaller crime groups knowing what has happened to the larger groups, you all can rest assured we are going to see some new alliances for self-preservation. Now, everybody off your asses! Go home, to debriefing, or to your next assignments! May God have mercy on your souls!"

Turning away from the podium and opening his hands to offer the microphone, "Father Leo."

Chapter 22

"See you in two days Rog. You got some wild plans for your time off?" Chomyn asked over her shoulder as we slowly shuffled our way through the sea of people in the smoke-filled meeting hall.

"Nope, just going to unwind and spend some time with Gabriel, just the two of us."

"Good stuff, it's nice to see a man who's not a complete asshole once and a while."

"Yeah, you have a good weekend too."

Chapter 23

I stopped at Adam and Emelia Burjour's house as usual to pick up Gabriel, and ended up staying for supper, again.

"This silence is driving the whole continental command, as well as regular forces absolutely fucking crazy."

"Adam, watch your tongue in front of the boy here, he repeats everything you say." Emma glared at her husband from across the small table. For a bear of a man, Momma had control of the den. "I'll feed him, Roger; you boys talk 'quietly' in the other room." She was good to me and Gabriel. She insisted on looking after him for me during my shifts, day or night, and absolutely refused any sort of payment. She always fed me when I arrived and always had leftovers of some sort tucked away in Gabriel's diaper bag for "her two" boys.

"Come on Ellis, we've been told. Let's go into the living room and see if there's a game on or something."

As I followed Adam into the living room, on the way past Gabriel sitting in his booster seat, I bent to kiss his head. My little man smiled at me, wide-eyed and trusting, his face filthy and trying to manage a fork full of spaghetti on his own. I leaned over and kissed Emma on her forehead. "Thanks for being here for us Emma."

She smiled and laid her hand over mine on her shoulder and patted it. "You and Gabriel are family, and family helps each other...enough. Get in there before he starts..."

"Ellis, get your ass in here...my beer's empty! Get yourself one too on your way!" Emma smiled and waved a mock backhand toward the other room where Adam was.

"Coming El-Capitan!" I cracked open the two beers, sucked the foam off of one of them as it started to overflow, and went into the small living room off the kitchen. The television was already on and Adam was scowling at the thing.

"Dammit, there's nothing but shit on tonight! Now there's a surprise, bah!" He pulled himself to the front of his easy chair and I knew he was going to say something profound "Everything is too quiet. I don't like it. It's fucking spooky."

"So what are you telling me this for?" I took a swig of my beer.

"I'm telling you this because there's an opening in regular forces right now and I can get you in no problem."

"Like I said, why are you telling me this?" I was starting to think he was going senile at this point.

"You stupid shit. Don't you see? Right now, Deev Squads are going to be preferred targets."

"Yes, and so are regular forces. Regular forces won't be hunted like you guys. There's word out that the big guys are putting prices on confirmed kills of any Deev member, even at home!"

"Adam, keep your voice down!" Emma kicked the swinging door open long enough to shoot him a look that would melt ice.

Over his shoulder toward the kitchen, "All right, all right." Looking at me again, "Ellis are you getting anything I'm saying?" He really was serious.

"Hey, don't worry about me I'll be fine. To be honest, I don't want to do anything else." His concern was confusing me, where the hell was this coming from?

"Ellis…Roger, please. Look in the kitchen at those two people. The boy needs a father, and Emma needs a…"

"Son!" Emma finished from the kitchen.

"You've got mighty stretchy ears woman!"

"Watch your step old man, the couch still has a soft spot for you. I don't!"

Shaking his head in defeat. "Anyways, before we were so rudely interrupted, they," pointing over his shoulder toward the kitchen with his thumb, "No, actually 'we' don't want to lose you. You know Emma and I never had children of our own and you're the only good thing we have in our lives. It's been wonderful since you and Gabriel came to us, and if placing you in regular forces keeps you alive, all the better for all of us." The look in his face was almost comical. In the time I have known Adam, I had never seen him show concern like this.

"This is not something I can decide on right now, I need some time to think about it." Deev was my vent, my soother. I was afraid to tell myself let alone anyone else that I enjoyed the hunting, and the righteous kill. Maybe that kept me in balance.

"You do that Roger, and I will make goddam sure a spot is held for you come hell or high water." He patted my leg and then got up to go to the kitchen and held the door for Gabriel.

Emma looked up from wiping Gabriel's face and snuck me a smile and a wink. These people were too good to be true. She let Gabriel down from the spaghetti-laden booster seat. "Go see your daddy," she said as she patted his bum and laughed.

Gabriel came screaming into the living room arms in the air like some wild chimpanzee, and then up to me in the chair, "Up Daddy!" I picked him up and tried to hug him, those always made me feel whole again, but just as quick he wiggled out and tried going down to the cat curled up on the floor. "I want the kitty! Let me down."

"Give me a kiss first you little twerp." He gave me a half-assed kiss and then proceeded to squirm out of my hold to terrorize the cat back in the kitchen. "Oh well, that beats nothing I guess." Boy he was sure getting old quick. It was like yesterday when....

"What's the matter Ellis, you all right?" Sam asked.

"Yeah, Adam I'm fine. It's that damn cat and my allergies." Bullshit yes, but it beats letting them know I was crying! They'd be all over me smothering me with love, making a fuss for no reason. To this day they still think Gabriel is mine, and really know nothing else of my family life. "We'd better get going now, it's getting late. Gabriel, come on buddy time to go."

On our way out the door I gave Emma a hug, and gave Adam an envelope. "What's this, I told you I didn't want any money…"

"No. I want you two to do me a favor. If anything ever happens, everything is in there for you, Adam, and Gabriel. I hope you don't mind; you guys are the only family I have."

They looked at me stunned and then Emma and Adam, both grabbed me and Gabriel in a hug. "Roger, we would be honored, but nothing is..."

I waved Sam off and gave Emma one last hug, and then Gabriel and I turned and left.

Chapter 24

"Back at home again little man, let's get you to bed." He was fast asleep on my shoulder, had been since we stepped onto the Mag-train to come home. I kicked off my shoes, threw Gabriel's bag on the floor beside the closet, and my clearance tag in the tray by the door that was full of months' worth of junk from my pockets. I walked into Gabriel's nursery. "Messages replay, nursery," I said to the apartment computer.

In a soft motherly voice, "three terminated connections, and one message, replay?"

"Replay." I rolled Gabriel out of his jacket and into his bed. "Rog, Rog, get out, it's more than you think." "End of message." I went numb again and froze for an instant. I hurriedly tucked Gabriel in and kissed his forehead, momentarily caught up in his beauty, then came back to realize there it was again. Could someone be playing a trick on me?

Chapter 25

"Christ Ellis your eyes look like piss-holes in the snow!" I only heard buzzing from Snake's mouth while we were riding in the transport to our location. "Rog…Roger," Waving his hand from the seat across the transport at me to try and snap me out. "What the hell is wrong with you, you're out to lunch today!"

"What, oh sorry. What was it you were saying Snake?"

Snake now looking at me with a bit of concern, "What's the problem Ellis?"

"Nothing, nothing at all…all is good." I forced a token smile for all to get off of my back.

"Location in four minutes," the voice sounded over the intercom. The transport drivers never knew the names or faces of the squads they were hauling, and the squads never knew the drivers. We could walk by each other in the street and never know otherwise.

I stood up, "All right boy and girls, let's load up and get ready to roll on signal!" The adrenalin really took me. The anticipation of the hunt and kill brought me back. The transport slowed to a stop and then the cell motors stopped. We heard a loud strike on the outside mechanism for the back door, followed by muffled footsteps running away on gravel. I looked up to the others, and they all looked up at me as well, confused, half done prepping their equipment.

"What the…that wasn't four minutes, that wasn't even one." Suddenly it dawned on me, "Get the fuck out now!" I frantically tried opening the door, and sure enough the mechanism had been jammed from the outside. The inside of the transport became chaos and screaming as we tried to break out the back door. The shitty thing about the transport is that it is also bullet proof, so blowing the back door off was definitely out of the question. "Fuck!" Two quick kicks to the doors did nothing, but the pain was sobering. "Calahoo, blow out the front cab! Everyone else open your mouths so the percussion doesn't' blow your fucking eardrums out!!" Instantly, she took a string of bullets into her rifle and set it on automatic and then the front wall disintegrated in a matter of seconds. Frantic, we all kicked at the remains of the front wall screaming and cursing knowing something was going to happen to the transport, just what and exactly when we did not know! The wall finally gave way into the cab. "Move!! Take your helmets and guns and get the fuck out!" Panic welling up in me as one by one they stumbled over the remains of the cab wall and out the driver's door, which stood wide open. I stumbled out after the everyone was finally clear of the truck and sprinting for cover.

"Ah Mr. Ellis." An unusually calm voice called from nowhere stopped us dead in our tracks. Common sense told me to get as much distance between me and the transport as possible.

"Mr. Ellis, please do stop. Ladies and gentlemen of Deviance Squad Six, all of you please." I stopped and turned to see where the voice was coming from. I also noticed that the others had stopped and turned. We had at least twenty meters between us and the transport. "Thank-you for stopping, it would be a shame to waste another innocent life." A lifeless body was thrown from the roof and landed with a sickening thud immediately to the left of the transport. By the uniform, I could tell it was the transport driver. His face somehow was looking down at the small of his back, blood clearly coming out of his eyes, ears, and nose. "Thank you. Now that I've gotten your attention, I would like to introduce myself. I am Jonas Eihner. Splendid fighter you are but it seems I have an advantage here on my side, come here my dear. Mr. Ellis, meet dear Alle. After all of these years in my service, I must tell you she's one of the best decisions I have ever made. Alle has made a wonderful addition."

From where I stood, I could tell it was her, even amongst the other three shadows standing in the street in front of a five and dime. I started to walk forward.

"Don't Ellis, they could be baiting you." Snake's attempts at holding me back were futile. I shook my arm free and he and the other two got the message to leave me to go.

"Alle." I kept walking slowly, steadily toward the storefront straining to see her. "A little late for seeing if I'm okay isn't it, Rog?"

"Stop right there, Mr. Ellis, I am about as comfortable as I can this close to a death squad member. Anyway, before I so rudely interrupted myself Deviance Squad Six, I have a little message for your superiors from our organization. Now, all of the general housekeeping as your sorts like to call it, has really cut into our business. It has been very difficult to be profitable when there is a major drain on our customers and merchants alike, let alone trying to find good replacements for stock that doesn't sell. It's gotten to the point where the 'enemies of my enemy' approach has come together and is working quite well to pool resources. This idea has been very healing for our groups. We still will be happy to go back to the way things were prior to all of this being blown out of proportion, or we could chip away at you and your sister forces and bring an unprecedented state of civil unrest to this continent. Who will police when the police are gone? Please be sure to tell someone with a sense of responsibility. This meeting will self-destruct in ten seconds." Calmly, he turned with the other shadows to leave. Out of the corner of my eye I saw dozens of shadows on the rooftops of the buildings around us, highlighted only by the lights of the city center, stand with their rifles to leave as well.

I turned to run and screamed, "Everyone get the fuck down now!" Just as the final word left my lips, the van exploded in a huge ball of flame that sent me and the other three ass over tits onto the pavement. The roar of the explosion dulled to the slow din of the fire, all I could do was lay there on the cold ground and appreciate the warmth the fire gave off, of all the stupid things while my ears rang and bled, and my head spun inside a tornado.

"You guys okay," Chomyn asked quietly of the two as if she was afraid to be louder and break something fragile.

"Yeah, I think so."

"Ditto," Snake mumbled.

"Ellis, how about you? You okay…Ellis…Ellis!"

"Grab my helmet and call central, and leave me alone here for a while okay."

"You all right or what, can you move…"

"I'm fine, just do it! Please, I've just seen a ghost." Chomyn grabbed my helmet from beside me, shot me a dirty look, and then walked away to the burning transport muttering something about stupid men. "Deev Six to central."

Chapter 26

"Ladies and gentlemen, we have a serious situation here. We have a potential for a guerilla war on our hands if we don't play our cards right, and could slip back to a worse place than where we came from only a few short years ago. To me, the answer is fairly simple: fuck them!" Slamming his hand down on the podium. Wilner glared around the room. Someone at the back of the room started clapping slowly, building in both numbers and speed until soon everyone else in the room joined in, finally bursting into screaming, whooping, fists pumping in the air, and whistling. John Wilner looked proud enough to burst. His toothy grin ate his whole face up. "All right, all right! Enough, come on now I got things to say." Slowly the room calmed itself, all Wilner could do was look around the room again, his timing was perfect, feeding us off of the enthusiasm captured in the room. Everyone in this room had their lives touched in one way or another by the violence and corruption that had infested our streets for so long, and everyone here finally realized the time was now! "We are at a very important crossroads and we must ask ourselves whether or not the collective 'I' am willing to ultimately make the greatest sacrifice of myself for my family, my friends, and their future? The reason I ask this of you is because the final step before the new beginning is going to be the most risky. Undoubtedly, there will be losses on both sides, but for the greater good! We must be sure we are totally committed in-spite of the danger and losses, or we will fail and never get another chance. Those of you who would like out, we respect your decision, and you have served well to this date and will be transferred to standard forces with seniority as it stands. Anyone interested please stand and go with Officer Lang to process the procedure." I lowered my head so I wouldn't have to see anyone leave, their leaving would be my own personal embarrassment. I didn't hear anyone shuffling or chairs sliding out of the way. I slowly looked up to see smiles growing on everyone's faces around the room. "Am I to assume by the mad rush to Captain Lang that I have everyone here still? Man, you people are sure dumb! Captain Lang, get the hell out of here! We have no use for you at the moment!" Laughter and chaos filled the room in an oddly jubilant sort of way, despite its morbid reality. "All right boys and girls, if we are going to roll, you have to listen good!"

Chapter 27

It had been several weeks and hardly anything had come to pass of interest. The regular runs were all still there, but certainly not in the frequency as it had been before. All of the squads had been practically tripping over one another trying to get some action on these cases in order to simply not to go stir crazy. In several cases, two or three squads would show-up at a single event. "Wholly shit, I never thought I would be saying this, but I am one bored girl tonight. Let's see your dick Snake. Show us Mister Scabs." Chomyn's face lit up in the night lighting a cigarette. Exhaling, "I'm sure a good laugh would make me feel lots better." Lately, when Chomyn and Calahoo got bored, they liked peeling the skin off of any man to make him feel dirty.

"Ha, ha, funny!" Grabbing at his crotch in defiance. Chomyn responded in-kind, simulating masturbating, and throwing it. Gross!

A huge explosion flashed up the night from a few blocks away from where we were patrolling. Then came the loud thunder of the gun blast. It was a big one!

"Wholly fuck! Ellis to Central, gun shots at Hedworth's Block. Deev Six responding. All right, helmets on and visors engaged. Chomyn, you and Snake use your scramblers and take the first shot! We don't want to liquefy him with the hit guns, all right? Let's go, night vision, infrared on, sweeping formation." We spread out slowly up the street, leapfrogging one another, while the other three were backing the one moving up. Another small explosion, and then shouts, close enough to hear but too far to make anything out.

"Deev One to central, officers down! Repeat officers down! Suspect has large caliber rifle, unknown size launching explosives. Scramble medical to Southam Block, north face stat, three officers down." The woman's voice sounded awfully controlled as Central broadcast all of that over all of headsets in the field.

"Establish frequency to Deev Squad One."

"Frequency open to Deev Squad One." The helmet's voice, even for a moment, was an anchor.

"Deev One, this is Captain Ellis of Deev Six, what is your position and status?"

"Sergeant Ellis, this is Private Morovitch. Sergeant Ames is down and out sir!"

"What is the situation with the runner?"

"The runner just walked into the area. We took immediate cover once we saw his gun, or whatever the fuck it is, and he just let a couple of rounds off. One just by dumb luck took out Sergeant Ames. Officers Singh and Cooper are injured but alive, out cold though."

"Man, this guy is fucking crazy!" Laughing in disbelief.

"What do you mean?"

"Are you in the area Sergeant?"

"Yes, e.t.a. two minutes. Can you hold on until we arrive?"

"Roger that. He doesn't know our position, but he knows we are here and I can't get a shot off because my shoulder is chewed-up from that last volley."

"Roger that. We will come-in from the south, two to the east of the building and two to the west. Advise your team to keep any fire away from those approaches. Where are you located?"

"I'm in the pile of garbage out the back door of the restaurant, disguised as a bleeding cop in black. The others are covered adequately as long as they don't come to!"

"Lie low, en route." I said looking over a dumpster at the side of the road with my rifle watching Calahoo skitter down the street, then Snake after her. Seeing them off, Chomyn and I went our own way. We finally came around the corner after assuring ourselves through the scanning and sweeping that our side of the building was clear. We slowly turned the corner still keeping our cover behind a cement stairwell into an old abandoned clothing shop, saw Snake and Calahoo and signaled okay. "See him anyone?" I asked over the headset.

"You fucks, I know you're all out there! I can feel you." He started to tail off as he came out of the shadows and threw part of a six pack of beer at no one in specific, falling on his ass in the process. How did he know we were here, and what the hell had he been taking?

"Magnify image five times." I said into the helmet quietly, but I think I could scream into the helmet and the dickhead probably not hear me.

"Wholly shit. Calahoo, I think I've found mister right for you." Everyone else must have magnified, judging by the giggling coming over the headset.

"Sir, I was about to say this man must make you homesick."

The runner/drooler, had his sinuses drain for some time down his face and into his long stringy hair, which was trying to blow in the wind, save the sticking.

"I'm sure some parts are worth salvaging." As soon as I said that, the runner was up and off like a bat out of hell running for his life with his gun over his shoulder, screaming on the top of his lungs like some animal.

"What the hell is this asshole on? Ellis to Central, runner heading north on foot. Request backup ASAP!" Screaming into the headset as I went into a sprint after him.

"Deev Twenty-Seven to Six, come in." "Come in Twenty-Seven." Huffing and puffing over the headset, Twenty-Seven was en-route somewhere.

"This is Captain Rana; we are landed about seven blocks north of your first location and coming in on foot doing a sweep of the area as we close in. Do you want us to hold off or can we snuff him?"

"If he comes anywhere near enough to get a shot off, take it. We couldn't even get a bead on him before he took off. I tell you man, whatever he's on made him sprint like a fucking pro. We are doing a cover and sweep from the south. From this alleyway, the way he took off he can only end up right at your feet providing you hurry to location. Watch yourself, he's got one hell of a gun from a museum or something!"

"Roger that Six, see you at the runner this side with his toes up."

The screams of the ambulance's sirens as it pulled into the alleyway to join the first was almost drown out by the drone of its hydrogen cell motors.

"Snake, Calahoo, you two stay here and cover for the medical crew, anything weird, and you call immediately! Me and Chomyn are going to cover any back path for this asshole!"

"Roger that." They spread out to 180 degrees apart and then backed into the darkness, almost invisible in their black garments and visors.

"Let's roll Chomyn." We ran out of the alleyway northward sweeping for what seemed like hours. Suddenly, we heard footsteps coming in the distance!

"Chomyn, get your ass down," I hissed into the microphone. "Deev Six to Twenty-Seven, What is your location?" "Deev Six, we are almost out of alleyway, where the hell is the runner?"

"He should be at you any time. Take cover and have someone shoot a laser down the center of the alleyway."

A hair-thin laser materialized down the middle of the alley. Suddenly my stomach tightened into a knot. "We passed the sonofabich!" There was absolutely nowhere to hide between where Twenty-Seven had their asses planted and where we were. Somewhere along the way we passed him! "Twenty-Seven, come in…be advised we passed the runner on our end and lost contact! Snake, Calahoo come in."

"Big Daddy, what's all the commotion?" Snake was clearly bored and trying my patience.

"We passed the fucking runner!! Clear the ambulances out of there immediately! Chomyn and I are backtracking toward you, covering everything, and Twenty-Seven is coming up behind us for support."

"Roger that! Snake out."

We inched our way back slowly looking up on every building in every stairwell, in behind and into each dumpster and down on the…"Chomyn, did you look at or above street level on the first sweep?"

"Yeah, just like always, and you and I know we didn't see a thing, right?"

"Right, but I think we didn't take below into account."

"So what does that have to do with…shit! That greasy little prick! He isn't so out of it after all is he? I think there is a manhole up there about fifty meters or so." We kept our momentum up on foot, sweep and cover, cover and sweep.

"Helmet, list sewage access covers on our present coordinate within one hundred meters south."

"Transmitting and plotting coordinates. Single sewage access present approximately fifteen meters south on present course." We swept up to the manhole cover at the side of the curb just about the same time Snake and Calahoo did. I didn't think we had to explain anything once they saw what we were looking at. I squatted down to pull the cover off and instantly was kicked in the ribs, and fell on onto my ass.

"Stop!!!"

"Jesus man!! Captain Rana of Twenty-Seven I presume." I stood, straightened myself and outstretched my hand to shake his iron grip.

"Sergeant Ellis, nice to have met you before you blew your head off!" His tone was a little less condescending over the headset. "I was in Counter-Terrorism before this shit, and I brought my paranoia with me here. Just shift your ass over boys and let me have a peek in there."

Snake and I got up off the ground and made way for the old bird, and nodded our hellos to the other three members of Twenty-Seven.

"Sergeant, you and your crew take a look inside the vent slots, and you'll see why I survived my last assignment for twelve years." He stood up, handed me his flashlight and moved aside for me to have a look. Sure enough, there was a thin wire, about three times the thickness of a human hair attached to the underside of the manhole with a magnetized loop, going down into the blackness of the hole.

"Now judging by the way the wire goes down there, I'd say it's attached at the bottom of the hole to that crazy fucking gun you said he was waving around a while ago. Now we have two choices, call central to send in a bomb squad with all the toys wasting who knows how much time, or we can discharge this thing and go for him ourselves." Looking at me, decision was made.

"All right now, you all go take cover in behind something solid and I'll set it off!" We all ran for cover and waited. Rana knelt down in front of the manhole and dug in his hip pack for a few seconds then fiddled at the manhole flipping it open and clear of the hole in one movement. Instantly, he was up and running toward where I was kneeling and dove into a pile of garbage screaming at the top of his lungs. Before I had the chance to ask what he had done, I heard a sound like someone farting into a tuba, big side. I just stood and watched as a shadow about the size of a large pear launched out of the hole, mouth open just like the other dummies around me, except for Rana.

Rana screamed, "Well someone with a gun should probably blow the thing up in the sky before it comes down and takes us out!"

Screaming, "Calahoo, get a fix on that fucking thing with your rifle!"

"Twenty-Seven tie in too!" Rana commanded.

"Replay launch trajectory, direct and lock on rifle." I heard Calahoo over my set. Quickly I looked up to the general area and jerked my head back down to where I thought it should be and dug in for the possibility of a miss. Four shots, two in succession, and two at the same time. The ball exploded at about thirty meters off of the ground. The wasted shrapnel from the grenade came down harmlessly, spattering and clicking on the ground like hail.

We all jumped up and brushed ourselves off, dancing and swearing struggling to get the hot shrapnel off of us before it burned through our suits and into our skin.

"All right boys let's go, there's another entrance to the way about three blocks away, two other squads are en route watching the other two ways out. We'll have him cornered and flush him out. Ellis, nice working with you. I look forward to doing it again soon."

"Thanks Rana, I owe you one." I called to my group, "Come on you three, let's get our asses in the hole, stat!" We had some lost time to catch up on.

Chapter 28

"We are going to go as fast and quietly as possible on the footways at the side of the tunnel, full visor. Snake, take point," I rasped into the headset, "Acknowledge." Three 'Rogers' meant it was a go. The way was very tricky, as the footway was about a foot and a half wide, and to its side a slimy forty-five-degree slope into a three-foot wide, crotch-deep river of whatever unholy fluids people can force down their toilettes, mixed with surface street water. All of this wholesome goodness caused a fairly dense mist that killed any normal vision from about twenty feet on, not to mention the tunnel ceiling was quite low, so we had to switch our small equipment packs to our fronts, and still had to crouch.

After about ten minutes of silent running, "Deev Twenty-Seven in position."

"Roger that Captain Rana, DeCarlo and Twenty-Nine pulling up the rear in position confirmed, flush the runner out our way baby."

I thought I heard. I stopped and signaled the squad to stop, quiet. Holding a position not being able to fully stand up was murder, my legs and back muscles were screaming now! Up ahead I heard the splashing again, and now so did my crew, I could almost see their ears perk up in anticipation of catching the runner. I signaled for them to go down on their bellies on the side walkways and stay as flat to the ground as humanly possible, and I rotated my pack to my back also, went down on my belly hugging the embankment, and looked into the mist. As far as I understood, this sewer section ran in a straight line, yet when I looked into the fog with my visor, even with heat and infra-red sensors I couldn't see a fucking thing.

"Ellis," Chomyn came over the headset, "I can't see a thing and I've tried everything in this helmet. Wait, did you see that, Ellis? There it is again, a light. A small green light moving erratically – fuck Ellis! This sonofabich is wearing an insulated suit for cover, and he's got one of those damn insulating devices to cover him from our scramblers. Request making the light go red."

Something wasn't sitting right here, but logically, this made sense. "Granted."

She took aim and let a burst go off. Down he tunnel about fifty yards or so came a muffled scream, down went the green light, now red.

"Hit him again Chomyn!" I screamed, not mattering anymore because the element of surprise was obviously gone. We heard a splash just as the second burst went off. The prick went into the water, which was flowing by us at an increasing rate. It must be raining up on the surface streets now!

"He has to come right by us," Calahoo said jumping up from the embankment of the sewer onto her feet into the grime. She crouched forward as if she were ready to catch a grounder in baseball.

"How's the water honey, meet any of your old boyfriends in there?" Snake asked squatting on the forty-five at the side of the water.

Calahoo lunged out of the almost hip deep water to pull Snake in, and was instantly pulled back into the water right before our eyes. Her scream was cut short as she was pulled-under by the runner's hands.

Snake fell onto his back in shock. "What the fuck…no! Calahoo's down in the water!"

I was already up and scrambling downstream on the bank trying to outrun the current and guess where I thought I would be ahead of them, then I jumped in trying to cover the whole width of the sewer channel feeling for a leg or an arm. "Snake, call ahead to the other teams on the emergency channel and tell them the runner is in the water…" Calahoo came to the surface about ten feet upstream of where I was standing, clawing and fighting like a cat trying to get out of the bathtub, gasping wildly for air and something to grab. The runner came to the surface on her back grinning madly with his arm around her neck. He pulled her hair back from the front of her head and pulled her off-balance and back under. "Calahoo! Come to me, come on, come to me," I said screaming, then I felt a leg brush up against me. I grabbed it and pulled with everything I had, screaming, "Chomyn I got the runner! Calahoo must be downstream now! Snake, you get your ass in there too!" I pulled at the leg and then bent over to get a hold of the head, that's when the leg and the rest of the body came to life. The son of a bitch was playing possum. A sharp kick to my midsection was all it took to get my attention. I just about blacked-out from the pain, and fought to clear my head to come into a defensive position. He lunged out of the water at me and in one fluid motion had my head pulled back with his fingers in my eye sockets, and ripped my helmet off to open me for palm shots to my head. This guy was definitely not baked, he was a professional! The head shots were quickly taking their toll, and he was so focused on them I managed to get a swing back into his groin with a solid punch. Screaming, he let go immediately but fought to control his pain and focus. I had a few precious seconds to gather myself. I straight palmed the runner in the bottom of the chin. Pulling himself up again he growled maniacally, blood spraying out of his mouth as he did. I made another good hit to the side of his head, and he went berserk. I managed to block or deflect a good number of hits, and then saw out of the corner of my eye Snake dropping a sputtering and screaming Chomyn on the incline and starting to rush to my rescue, "Snake hold back!"

"All right enough fucking around now sweetie-pie," I said as I spat a gob of blood from my mouth. I rolled into the runner's chest dodging and deflecting out a punch, then came up cupping my hands and slamming them over his ears with everything I had just as he pulled his arm back to deliver a potentially good hit into my already swollen face. My father, may he rot in hell, always taught us to strike, disorientate, and kill. The runner fell back into the shit river holding his ears screaming blue murder and I staggered back from the exertion. "Get up...get up I said!" Gasping for air.

Ever so slowly he rolled his head up toward me, and let go of his ears. Smiling, he got up and advanced toward me, "You piece of shit, you just made the biggest mistake of your life! One pussy shot won't finish this any other way than you being taken out!" He jumped up and gave a beautiful roundhouse kick that might have connected had he not advertised as soon as he moved into it. I instantly dropped to my chin in the sewage to let his round house kick clear of where my head was, planted a flat fist shot into his crotch, and then sprung – up and kicked his planted leg collapsing it backward before he finished. He went down screaming into the water up to his waist, floating and trying to fight the current. Painfully, he stood up and looked at me as he hopped occasionally to keep his balance on his good foot.

"Well cop, come put the cuffs on me. You win." Spreading his arms, hands outstretched and his palms up to show surrender, smiling. This was simply surreal. Noticing my confusion, in an instant an ugly curved blade was in his hand already in motion for my neck. I barely had time to move out of the way of his swinging arm, which I grabbed and twisted behind his back and violently jerked it up until the popping noise came, dislocating and tearing his shoulder apart. Instantly he fell away into the water screaming, letting his now useless right arm hang down by his side. I walked around to face him.

"Now, who the fuck sent you to do this?"

"Fuck you." The runner spat through the blood and pieces of his teeth.

I kicked him in the jaw sending him backward into the flow. Talking obviously wasn't working. He slowly picked himself up out of the slime once again, his face advertising the pain. "Now, as I said before cop," gasping for air and composure, "Fuck you."

I was now furious at the arrogance of this man. I brought back my arm to strike the final blow for this asshole when I heard and felt the charge of a scrambler blaze right by me into the runner, dropping him instantly.

"What the fuck is going on here?" The river of shit was slowing down substantially, the rain had to have stopped for some time already, but it still managed to try to float the runner away. I bent down a grabbed a handful of the scruff of his hair as he started to float by me, and then stood there like some asshole in front of my two stunned officers. Thankfully, I was also looking at a shaky, shit-covered Calahoo, scrambler still pointed to where the runner had been.

"Calahoo, what the hell are you doing, I was in control of the situation?"

"Obviously not. I wish you could see yourself right now sir. Frankly, you're not yourself, and the runner is no good for scanning if his brain has been pounded into mush. I think you should take a few minutes to calm down before you do anything else at this point."

Point taken. I looked with my mouth hanging open to snake and Chomyn, as if to ask what they thought, but I could see by their faces they were just as shocked as Calahoo. Still gasping for air, I pulled the runner to rest on the side of the incline, "Here, you catalogue this asshole and make sure you clean the entry area for his skull." I walked down the tunnel maybe fifty feet to calm down and come back to earth again.

Chapter 29

"Well Mister Ellis, the runner you four neutralized last night was plugged in, and it seems we are getting information that leads us to believe the alliance we are fucking with is a little more involved than we were first lead to believe...more information to come." John Wilner scanned the room, which was deathly quiet. "Regrettably, last night we lost a few more good men and women, contributing members. That ladies and gentlemen, is one night; one night's statistics. Now, we need to take this situation down and fast. All of the kills are getting scanned and rescanned, reviewed and re-reviewed for anything that leads us to where the core of this starts. Out in the field we have to be aware of anything that might hint toward who is responsible for any of this shit, no clue is too small. If it looks like something, treat it as such. Trust your gut, it never is wrong!"

Chapter 30

Later that night at home, I sat on my bed. Wilner's words swirling in my head. I wasn't sure if the past few days' events were numbing me or if it was the scotch, I had been cuddling all night after putting Gabriel to sleep. "Where the hell is that asshole…" To myself, I called Snake over two hours ago.

"Harry Schlanker at the door," the angelic voice chimed. I jumped up and opened the door to Snake who was attached to an old lady style grocery pull-cart that was full of wires, buttons and hard-cases. There must have been three hundred pounds of that shit there. "What the hell did you bring?"

"You told me to bring everything I had for filtering, separating, and enhancing. Here it is so back off! You haul this up three floors by yourself in your cheap fucking shithole hotel or whatever the hell this is supposed to be? Besides, why the hell didn't you answer when I buzzed from downstairs to get some help?"

"I disconnected it a long time ago. It keeps the riffraff out."

"Ellis, I feel I can be frank with you outside of work where rank is meaningless. You are kind of a dick!" Snake pushed into my apartment still puffing, then put his hands on his knees, trying to catch his breath.

"Hey, what does this thing do?" I bent over and grabbed a little black box with wires and led lights, turning it over and over to see what it would do.

"Don't touch that, or anything else as a matter of fact!" He abruptly stood up and pulled it out of my hand before I could even figure out how to turn it on. "I love the fact that I can help you, especially on my free time, but please don't touch my stuff...at all." He raised his eyebrows to solidify what he just said.

I saluted and the and then walked into my kitchen, "What do you want to drink?" And we were off. After I tossed him a beer, I came back into the living room and flipped my wall screen on to the warm smile of the computer's prompt.

"Systems initialized, Mr. Ellis."

"Video and voice messages, archives please." I waited patiently.

"Loaded."

"Load all female voice messages within the last quarter." I looked at Snake, who wagged his tongue at me like, and then simply turned back to work on his pile of junk.

"Female video and voice messages, last quarter loaded."

"Run all." A picture of Emma flashed across the screen and she opened her mouth to speak. The next messages were pretty well the same. "Skip...skip...skip..."

Snake looked up from his boxes and wires shaking his head, "Do you not get any interesting messages, even wrong numbers?"

"Well it's obviously worse for you as I see you're her spending the evening with me."

"Yes, good point. It really is sad. Misery loves company. If two windows open at once, we have the option of the sweet release of death to meet us on the street together."

"Rog no I."

I heard and saw it again, I froze. "Snake, that's her! Turn on your fucking machine, that's her! There should be a second one there too!"

"Rog, get out, it's more than you think."

"That's the one!" My arms outstretched.

"Roger, settle down now. We've got her. She's not going anywhere. Tell your system to hold the message and we will dump it into my mixing bowl here," sweeping his hand over his pile of gadgets.

"Sorry. I lost myself and all but she is my sister and…" My voice trailed off. I sighed and brought my head up to face the computer, "Hold last two messages in audio and video, ready for copy to external lead per my voice only."

The computer did her stuff and a second later, "Loaded and holding Mister Ellis." Snake plugged his last lead into my computer and looked back and forth between the two machines as if to see some sort of interaction.

"Download complete." Sexy computer announced.

"Done. Next one Ellis?" We finally found the second one and dumped it also. "Now what I'm going to do here is take both messages, split the audio and video into two different entities and then run a nifty little program that finds any similarities in the audio note for note, as well as the video grain for grain that would combine in a pattern of any sorts to make a common image or audible sound that is any use to us."

"Snake, I take back most of the things I said about you behind your back, and some of the things I said to your face, you actually are useful."

"Thanks."

Chapter 31

"Ellis get in here; the program is finished." I jumped up from the couch where we had been watching old boxing matches of Mohammed Ali, my idol.

"Well, what did we find?"

"'We' found fuck all. 'I' found a couple of things." Pointing at his chest. "Let's just see…yup. Well, number one it is the same person, and she's wearing the same earrings in both messages…"

"Great, nice work. We find the earrings the mystery is solved."

"Patience my dear man, ah yes. Do you know this sound?" He pushed a button and I heard what sounded like an old-fashioned school bell being rung five consecutive times. "She deliberately fucked-up the transmission image of here so as to hide the origin of the call, but forgot scrub the entire audio."

"I know that sound, and it's going to drive me out of my mind if I don't think of it!" I started pacing around the room, ranting and raving but I just couldn't think of it. "Fuck!" I finally screamed-out in frustration.

"Hey boss, you're scaring me. How about you just go and get us a couple of more beers and by that time I may have found the origin of the bell. Okay?"

"That box can do that?"

"It cannot, I can. You just have to know how to ask and the world will be at your feet."

A few minutes later as I was coming back into the room with the beer, "Ding ding ding! Got it Ellis!" Snake was standing waving his arms in the air and doing an ass-waving victory dance as he looked at his monitor from on top of one of his boxes.

"Well?"

"Well, it seems sister is alive and well and working at the Stock Exchange right here in our wonderful city, yeeehaaaw! Start spreading the news…" His singing faded into a buzzing in my ears as he turned his back to me, and continued to poke and prod and tweak his computer junk.

My sister truly was alive and well! It was still beyond belief as it was, but working at the stock exchange? Why would she have been with the assholes if she had a legitimate job?

"Fuck me…" I couldn't help screaming and stomping around like a little kid in the mud.

"What, what is it, Ellis? What the hell is going on!!"

"She's working for the stock exchange."

"Yes, we already figured that out. Good for her, I hear they treat their people well."

"Listen and shut your trap for a second! She works at the stock exchange, say even at the lowest level a trader."

"And?"

"So, don't you see what's going on here? At the level of the stock exchange, depending on how many there are, they could be messing with the whole portfolios, funds, and if there's enough of them, whole economies. With their people in enough areas, they could pull the plug at any time, creating huge collapses and destabilization! More unemployment, more crime, more money, and more monopoly! The stock exchange is the means to their end!"

"Oh my God." Snake went pale.

Chapter 32

While our faces glowed in the monitor surveillance room, they zoomed in onto Alle. "There she is..."

"Okay, Snake, we have a camera and spotters on the floor everywhere to see what the hell Ellis's sister is buying and selling on a daily basis." Wilner looked skeptical as he looked at the monitors. "All right Goddamit, cue the traders."

"Onec Resources, 10000 shares here, all or none!" Two outstretched clapping hands rose out of the sea of screaming heads and flailing arms on the trading floor, and it began.

Another set clearly up in the air, and then another. Good, the three "shadow" traders were nicely triangulated around Alle, who was already focused with buying and selling for the day, out-screaming and out-pushing the male counterparts.

"Now we start the fun." Snake turning to his computer screen wringing his knuckles. "There we go. Global Federal Marketing, she's bidding ten dollars a share." Snake and the traders figured out a hand signal system based on binary code for speed and its difficulty to detect, it worked wonderfully. He started to type a response which would go in vibrating pulses in the same code to a personal pager on their hips. "I told them to bid up to twenty just to see what happens, and to get as many liquid shares possible. Man, I love shopping with someone else's money." Flashing a 'Cheshire Cat' grin over his shoulder to Wilner and me.

"You remember asshole, if you lose any of the funds to this fart in the wind you two schemed up, I'm going to cement your asses into the ground and park my bike in the cracks forever!"

The hours passed and with each of Alle's bid to buy, many were beaten, often only by a slim margin, or spoiled with a massive pullout just after the price was jacked-up. With some sales, Snake simply played around by having standing bids to buy all or none at a drastically reduced rate, in order to scare any potential buyers away or shave points off. Most of the time it worked, not always, but enough to put a wrench in the works and raise Alle's frustration level. The mounting stress clearly showed on her face more and more as the hours passed.

"Yahoo, I did it!" Snake screeched hands in the air.

My eyes shot open, I must have been dozing off waiting for something to happen in this stuffy little office above the trading floor, one of dozens.

"What, what…what the hell did you do?" Wilner screamed, now completely pissed at being woken as well.

"Gentlemen, I have just made five million dollars net for the federal treasury." Looking around the room at us, who were in total silence. "No need to thank me all at once." Turning back to his screen, "Assholes, I should get off of the tax shit for life…"

The clanging of the trading bell signaled the stop to another day's trading. Hands flew up and paper scraps were thrown up into the air and some cheers also went up. Alle stormed out through the crowd.

This continued for days, and Alle quickly figured out who the three men were that were stealing her bids. On the last day, once the bell was rung to cease trading, she stormed through the crowd directly to the closest of the three agents and straight-palmed him in the nose instantly breaking it, exploding blood everywhere. The agent screamed and fell to the ground holding his broken nose and trying to contain the blood that was pouring onto his coat. Alle kept walking right through not missing a beat.

Watching from the monitors, the whole group of us was in tears laughing at the agent on the floor who was finally cradling his bloody face in his coat. "Ellis, your sister turns me on, she has spunk!" Snake said looking over his shoulder at me still laughing hysterically.

Wilner was the first to stop laughing long enough to talk, "Now let's pray to God this goes as well as we hope."

Chapter 33

"Alle my dear, what in the world has gotten into you this week?" Jonas asked, sitting hands folded at his elaborate glass desk flanked by two immaculately dressed bodyguards.

Alle hadn't even finished storming into the office and threw her purse down into the leather couch by the door, still infuriated about the day and it's blundering. The question stopped her dead in her tracks as if she had just been slapped. "What...do you mean Jonas?" She knew.

"What I mean is every day for the past eighteen months we have had traders methodically gaining a majority foothold in our target companies to meet our goals, your goals too Alle! You had a good hand in getting us this far consistently, now out of the blue you have a..." Standing to lean forward on his desk with both hands forward like an animal ready to pounce, veins bulging in his forehead now.

Alle interrupted, "Jonas, you don't understand, you see every time that a bid..." Alle was scared now, totally fearing for her life. She knew that it hung in precious balance.

Slamming his fist repeatedly on the table, spitting as he screamed, his intensity was almost insane. "You had a bad fucking day, you poor thing-fuck you!! Do you know how many millions you cost us! Do you know how far we have gotten behind schedule with just you alone? You set us back weeks, with each single fucking day!" Pointing at her, "This happens once! Do you hear me, once! I took you under my wing. Who was a real father to you? Alle, answer me." Calmer now. Sitting back down in his chair, the tempest barely held back behind the eyes under the smiling face.

Shaking with tears streaming down her face, "You, you are the only father I know Jonas." Sobbing quietly, her voice fell to a feeble whisper.

"This is the first and last time Alle. We are so close. I will not jeopardize this for anyone or anything." Jonas, stood and came around his desk with his arms wide open to exaggerate his love for her. Slowly she went to him and was embraced, she had to.

Chapter 34

"Ellis, get the fuck back into position, she'll be back any second!" Snake's voice buzzed in my headset of my helmet.

"Shoo fly, don't bother me." Quietly I whispered back melodically. I was snooping, taking in all of the pictures on the walls of pretty people I didn't know. I carefully took one picture off-of the wall and turned it in my hand. The back, had never been opened. My heart sank as I realized I was looking at the picture that came with the frame. I glanced up at the other pictures and those perfect smiles and teeth all must have originated from the same story.

"Ellis, come on. Get the wires in and go!"

I put the picture back on the wall making sure it was meticulously straight. Creeping into the large bedroom, I went to the dresser and went through the drawers looking without trying to mess up her stuff to find anything of interest. I went to her nightstand, opened her drawer and there inside was a picture of me with a black eye when I was ten. The top right of it was charred. I remember the day so well; Dad was actually proud of my black eye and split lip. He was proud because I had won the fight with the older, stronger boy, and he would have to take a picture of me as a trophy to my becoming a man. My head was still swimming when he took it.

"Lifeguard on deck."

Shit! That was the signal that Alle was coming home. Snake patched the live feed of her onto my HUD in my visor. By the way she was walking, she clearly had one shitty day. "Visor off and retract," I said into the wire. The image flickered off the screen and the visor shield instantly retracted back into the helmet. I took another glance at the picture and my heart bled for the sad little boy in the picture, I barely remember being him. What a fucking weenie! I would go back and kick my own ass if I could. Pushing the drawer closed on the night table, I realized I must have stared at the picture a little longer than I had wanted to. I heard the deadbolts retract into the door. I was cornered in the bedroom still with no out. I sprinted to the closet and closed the door leaving enough of a crack for me to peek out of.

The front door kicked open and slammed against the wall, and then saw a purse leaving her hand and heard something glass shattering when it struck across the room. Alle was sobbing softly. She feebly closed and bolted the door behind her, and put her other bag on the counter in front of the pictures. She wiped her nose with the back of her hand, and as she wiped the smeared raccoon mascara more into her wet eyes, looked up at the pictures and froze, hand still at her eye. Slowly, she took her hand away from her face, reached up and adjusted the picture I had straightened. Shit! She straightened and came directly into her room. I could hear movement, and then I heard doors opening slowly. She was checking the apartment out!

Squatting, I struggled to get the tranquilizing charge inputted into the gun but in the dark I couldn't see the setting without the visor, and I couldn't put the visor down because the motor in the headset would bring her right to me instantly. Fuck it! The closet door swung open to Alle in boxer shorts, a T-shirt and an old issue revolver, shocked as shit to see me there, and frozen in-place.

It was all I needed. "Hello sis." I kicked her as hard as I could in the solar plexus, doubling her over while still trying to block with the hand that had dropped the gun. "I'm sorry sweetie, but it has to be like this now." I punched my sister in the side of the head, safely taking her down before she had the chance to gut me.

Chapter 35

"Did we get what we went for Ellis?" Bob Preen asked. He was commander from Deev 29, a bit of a weasel but very reliable and competent.

"Yep, here we are." I tossed him the gun Alle had tried to clear her apartment with. "Go do your magic boys."

Preen walked away bouncing the gun in his hand, feeling the weight and grip mumbling to his second in command as he walked away, something about loving a girl who could handle a gun this size.

What the boys had to do was go and take a pot shot at Mister Jonas, hitting something soft and non-vital, like his leg or his security guard. The intent was that the bullet would be retrieved, and identify Alle as the shooter. This would assure Alle into coming into the safety of our arms. I had just turned to leave headquarters when Snake came running up out of breath.

"Ellis, I just heard Alle's apartment complex has been leveled. All six floors destroyed with everything and everyone in them. Four Deev teams and specialty services headed out there once they heard whose residence it was. Ellis, we saved her life."

All I could think of was that her life was saved, not that there were probably dozens of families torn apart, or even decimated. "We better put a hold on Preen until intelligence gets done. If Jonas thinks she's gone, we have things even easier all around."

Chapter 36

"Roger, untie me you fuck!" There she was, slurring, moaning, and weakly trying to fight out of the restraints and sedatives she was given as a precautionary note during the night.

I fully expected to see her rip her restraints off, and stand-up to kick the shit out of me. "I think it's best we keep you like this until we bring you up to speed on what's going on here."

"How about some water then, can you manage that?"

Smiling, "Yeah, I think I can arrange something." I got up and went to the nursing station, and then came back with the water.

"Untie one hand at least, so I can drink from a glass half-assed at least."

"Nope, I got you a straw to use. Here, I'll hold it for you." I held it to her mouth and she drank deeply. "You keep forgetting you used to kick the shit out of me, and I've been pain free for a while now. I've grown fond of not being bruised."

Looking right at me, I could hear the gears going in her head, "You still practice, Rog?"

"That's like asking if I still breathe. Yes, almost every night. I have my own dojo. It's small and I can't put some of the weapons out because of Gabriel…" I trailed off, smiling suddenly thinking about him.

"Gabriel? You have a kid Rog?" She threw her head back and laughed, then instantly tried to curl into a ball moaning in pain from the kick to her ribs. "Wow, I'm an auntie…show me a picture. Boy or girl?" "It's a boy. He's the best thing that ever happened to me." Holding up a picture I fished out of my pocket.

"Good looking kid Rog. He's lucky he looks nothing like you. Where's his mom?"

"She died right after he was born." The tone I used caught Alle off guard and she knew not to ask again.

"Fuck…so, why the hell am I here all tied up, I have to log in soon or they will think something is going on."

"As far as they are concerned, you are dead." Maybe I was a little too blunt.

"What the hell do you mean dead? What the fuck did you do??" Now she was awake and pulling at all of her restraints, every vein was bulging in her face and arms.

"Well more specifically, blown-up. It seems some 'freak accident' with my hands up making quotation marks, has leveled most of what was above or below your apartment."

She relaxed, and fell back into her bed with her mouth falling open onto her chest. "The whole goddam apartment complex…why the hell…!" She started sobbing. "He wanted me, why the hell did he level the whole fucking place, you know how many kids were in there!" She turned her face away from mine, quietly fighting one last time against the restraints, and then went limp, crying softly.

I got up to shut the hospital door. "Alle, you have to believe me, it wasn't us. We don't operate like that, we are 100% surgical, if we want one person, we don't take out the whole block. We think it was the Brotherhood…"

"No it was the Brotherhood, and if you hadn't kidnapped me, I would be dead right now, or one month from now when I contacted you guys everything, I had been gathering on them." That hit like a ton of bricks.

"Is that why you contacted me at home then, you wanted a way out?"

"Yes. I knew some of the people within Deviance were corrupt, I never could find all of the names, and so I contacted you. Even after all these years you thought I was dead, probably scared the shit out of you, didn't I?" Turning to me now, smiling a wicked smile.

"I thought I was going crazy." I patted her arm and got up, "I have to go now, we have you listed here as a psych patient so no one will bother you. There's a guard to sit with you in case anything goes down." I opened the door and the agent was already there to my surprise.

"Agent Reiss sir." He outstretched his hand and shook mine in an iron grip. This man was an ape. I told Alle goodbye and said I would see her tomorrow; I just wish I would have taken time to think about what her smile meant.

Chapter 37

"What the fuck do you mean she's gone?" I screamed into the screen of my computer.

"Daddy, that's a bad word, you can't say that," Gabriel said as he climbed into my lap. Dammit, I forgot I had days off and his ears were open as usual! I put him back down onto the floor, "Go find your cars buddy." I shook my head and smiled briefly. Turning back to the screen, my voice down ten notches I hissed, "What the hell do you mean she's gone?"

"Hey, don't shoot the messenger! All I know is central sent a guy in for guard duty with all the right credentials, yes plural credentials, and sometime during the night they both disappeared. I checked with records and apparently this Reiss guy was a part of a deviance division. It took me all night to figure it out, and after tearing his file apart I finally found he didn't exist at all, anywhere before nine o'clock last night. He was planted Rog. Planted from high-up, and from within." Snake trailed off.

I just stared into space. The safest thing I could reason is that she played me for a fool. I let my guard down!

"Rog…Rog, you all right man?"

I shook it off. "Yeah, I'm okay. Hey, is there any way you can find out where and who inputted the Reiss file?"

"Why, Mr. Ellis, do you take me for a big dumb stupid-head? It was inputted at a Mill's area library computer terminal. You know, the ones that are on line for only finding old books and newspaper entries anywhere in the city, and it was entered using some central geek's passcode. His name is Nicholas Vorencotta. He's really greasy, I met him once before."

"Snake, I love you." I got up and started to run to get dressed. "Oh, by the way, pick me up at the subway depot in two hours, south-end. That way I'll have time to drop Gabriel off. We have some visiting to do."

Chapter 38

"I honestly don't know what you're talking about," Nick Vorencotta said nervously as he adjusted his freshly bent glasses. Apparently, it happened when his apartment door was accidentally kicked open, then shut onto his head a couple of times, then the fingers on his non-dominant hand once, by accident. At least his nose stopped bleeding. Snake had some serious interrogation training where he came from, with a personal touch of sadism.

"Now seriously, Nicholas…Nick, you are one of a handful that has clearance access to records and resources within Deev. Why and how did you enter this asshole into the system?"

"Rog, want a beer?" Snake had already found the fridge and it was well stocked, and I mean really well stocked.

"No thanks."

"Nick, you single?" Snake asked just as I was going to jump in again. I saw him wink at me, letting me know he was taking the reins.

"What do you mean?"

"This is a pretty simple yes or no question, are you single? I mean a guy like yourself living alone and all, with a fridge stocked like that either has a good woman, or is a homo. Are you a fag Vorencotta? It wasn't listed when I checked into your personnel file, but I can put it there." I held back a smile. This was true entertainment.

"NO!! I mean no, I'm not gay. I just like to entertain every now and again."

"What do you mean entertain? Do you strip down and have a woman giggle at that dumpy body of yours with its bluish-white skin? A guy like you must have a big dick because I really can't see much else going for you."

"As a matter of fact, I am quite well known for having a…"

I jumped right in, "Gross, stop! You pay a girl well enough and she will tell you what you want to hear. Am I right or what?" Looking right at Snake.

"Hey, why was that question directed at me?" Shaking his head at me, he threw me a beer and I opened it and took a long draw. "I predict Nick, that you have had the service of a prostitute, probably several over the years. That is an offense nowadays? You could lose your job, your credibility…and your pension. How many years do you have in now, fifteen, twenty maybe?" Nick was obviously nervous, literally squirming now on the kitchen chair. "Jesus, right at the finish line too with only a few yards to go."

"Now wait, what do you want? I mean a guy gets lonely and all, is that something to create a fuss about?"

"Nick what we would like to know, all bullshit aside, is if you created an identity within the Deev system within the last 24 hours?" Nick put his broken, bloody hand up and started to say something. I pointed right at him, "No bullshit remember, one chance!" I went to poke a bone sticking out of one of his fingers.

"Alright, alright." He pushed up his bent glasses and smeared the lenses with his fingers in an attempt to clean them. "I had a woman in early yesterday morning, to do a few services, a wonderful little redhead who…"

I was really getting annoyed at the details now, "Christ sakes man get to the point, I don't want to hear the whole fucking thing!"

"This redhead, well I paid her and then put my wallet on the table by the door, and she offered me a quickie for the road. I laid in my bed while she left and when I finally got up, I realized she took my wallet along with my encryption codes I was given when I moved into intelligence years ago. I even encrypted my encryption codes to the point of being unbreakable. I guess I was wrong."

I almost felt sorry for Nick. "Well, good thing she didn't take your whole hand to use your pass scanner to gain access, you never know where your hands have been. Now let's make a deal. You tell us where to find this lovely Irish lass, and we'll not report any of this. Fuck-us over, and we'll have you and your exploits all over the front of everyone's computer screen for the morning news, and you will be typing with a pencil."

"The name she goes by is Banzai. She's high-end, it took me four months to save-up for her."

"Where do we find her then? Where's her walk?" We needed to get going.

"Off of the Cathedral on Fifth. Every time I've seen her, she wears a green coat, fabric's always different, but it's always green. Hey, you guys will forget all of this like you said?" The look of fragile hope on his face was almost sad.

"Yes of course." He slouched back in his crappy vinyl kitchen chair and sighed as if a big weight was lifted off of his shoulders. "That is until we ever need something else." We smiled and got up and left, closing the door behind us.

Chapter 39

It was a good thing Snake had a fuel cell car, because it would be damn hard to take an irate hooker anywhere against her will if needed on the public transport system. Even in the car, it took the better part of three hours to cross the city. Finally we arrived and toured the cathedral block up and down, over, and over…and over.

"Pull in here Snake and I'll buy us each a coffee."

"You cheap prick! How do you get away with that when I paid for dinner?"

"Decaf for you it is."

"Lots of cream and sugar," he screamed after me through the open passenger window as I crossed the sidewalk to the kiosk. I got the goods and then turned to glance back while paying to see a stunning redhead in a green coat leaning in the passenger window of Snakes car. As I approached, she stood up.

"Hi, is one of those for me?"

"Yeah, this one's white and sweet, just like you." I smiled my biggest smile and handed her Snake's coffee.

"Thanks for the coffee asshole! Why didn't you give her yours?" Snake muttered more under his breath.

"Yes, thanks." She hugged the coffee in both hands to draw its precious heat into her, buried in the monstrous green fur coat that was part Grinch and part mountain gorilla.

"This is Banzai Rog, and by the way she's not Japanese. She says two thousand for two at once, or fifteen hundred for one at a time."

"Well, how much just to talk." I asked looking right into her green eyes. This was truly one stunning animal and I felt unhealthy feelings just looking at her.

Her business smile soon turned to a scowl. "I don't make money to talk, and I don't have any interest in talking to you, so you and your fucking cop friend here can just leave now!" She threw the coffee down in the street and started to storm-off.

I grabbed her wrist before she could get away and pulled her around. All of a sudden, I saw the prettiest stars floating around in my head, and instantly was on the ground feeling shoes being kicked into my ribs, then it stopped.

"Ellis, help!" I managed to look up from the ball I had collapsed into and saw Snake trying to choke out a very large man with no neck! Slowly I pulled myself up to my feet, keeping my distance until I caught my breath. "Ellis, any time now!" He was getting somewhat frantic riding the man's back and clearly losing his grip. The ogre was getting antsy and started hitting him with the back of his head and then slamming into a brick wall backward, with Snake hanging on for the whole ride.

I looked down the street in time to see Banzai in her green gorilla coat running toward a limousine to hide, obviously waiting for her sidekick/chauffeur who was busy right at the moment. I had to end this quickly. I ran up to the ogre and kicked him in the groin. Both he and Snake looked very stunned, neither moved. I kicked him so hard I thought bells would go off in his eyes when his nuts reached them…no response. He lunged out to hit me. I grabbed his arm and spun around his back while Snake bailed, and drove the ogre to the ground head-first, dislocating his shoulder and knocking him out. He didn't make a sound, he just laid there with his ass up.

"I guess he put his arm out to break his fall. Technically I didn't use excessive force because it was self-defense, he could have fallen on me." I heard movement down the street as Banzai bailed out of the limo and was high-tailing it away on foot. "Banzai, stop! If you want tiny here to ever play the piano, you'll come back and talk! All I want is to talk!" She looked at the way I had his fingers in a bunch twisted around his back with his arm and realized his well-being was worth something.

"All we're gonna do is talk right, and then you'll let him go, and me?" Walking cautiously toward us.

"Yes, I promise. Snake, you okay?"

"Yeah, but I sure could go for a coffee. Oh I forgot; a hooker's comfort is more important than my comfort!"

"Female companion asshole!" Walking right by Snake in complete disgust.

"Yes, in the grand scheme of things the female companion is presently number one, but you're a close second." I helped Snake up as he brushed himself off and checked his nose for blood, over and over again. "Come on Banzai, a little closer so at least we don't have to announce to the world what we're doing, or do you want me to ruin the area for business for you?" Holding my hand up, "Alright, close enough. Your brick shithouse is okay. His shoulder is just dislocated, not broken." I let his massive hand slap to the ground.

"What do you want from me?"

"I want my coffee you psycho bitch!" Banzai gave him the finger.

"Do you remember a male client by the name of Nicholas Vorencotta?" I asked as I hopped up to sit on a closed dumpster beside the still sleeping ogre.

Smiling. "Yes, an unusually boring looking fellow, but he was very gifted in the…I actually considered charging him half." I could see the devil in her eyes.

"Again, gross! How about we keep that type of information inside your head! Now, how about the little issue of his wallet going missing." Snake checked his nose for blood again as he asked.

"I have no idea of what you're talking about." She was very cool.

I stepped on the goon's pinkie finger with the heel of my boot – CRACK! Looking at her. "Does that seem to jog your memory? Every time you feed us a line of shit, another piggy dies. You have nineteen more lies before we move to breaking other things here. Tu comprendes?" I stepped back to let Snake continue.

She finally let out a muffled scream from her covered mouth, shaking visibly. I couldn't tell if it was from anger or fear. "Alright," sighing heavily and looking down composing herself, "Alright! They told me if I picked Nick up and took his wallet, they would pay me double of what I would make in the trick, and forgive my gambling debt. I can't refuse that kind of deal." She looked sincere enough.

"Who might THEY be?" I started to get a little jumpy standing there doing nothing, so I started to shift from side to side.

"Wait!" She screamed holding both hands up in the air to stop me. "Two men. They picked-up the wallet, gave me the money, and let me get away with the debts cleared. I had to phone them to tell them I had gotten the wallet."

"Do you remember the number or the names of the two men?" Snake asked while checking his nose again for blood with the back of his hand.

"They didn't give me their names, but Günter my personal phonebook would remember the numbers to call, but he broken right now," she said as she pointed to the lifeless monster on the ground.

Chapter 40

"You two pinheads have nothing better to do on your days off than this?" Wilner was some shade of pissed-off. "The only thing you two got was some stolen cell number, and a possible brutality charge."

"Hey, that's not fair, the guy punched me blind side, and then screwed up Snake's good looks, I had to put him down. I thought he pulled a knife!"

"Am I supposed to buy this shit?"

"Just give me the benefit of the doubt, I need a frequency tracker to find the cell. I find the cell, maybe I find the contacts, simple."

For the first time today, he didn't look at me as if I was a total idiot. "Ellis, you're a total idiot. You're lucky any lead on this Brotherhood bullshit I want flogged to the point that it is dead. You two go down to the tech room and requisition whatever fucking toy is needed for this cell tracking, have them call upstairs to me for authorization."

Chapter 41

"What would you gentlemen like today?" I expected a complete geek to be running this room, but the guy looks like Mr. Universe. To hear the technical nonsense coming from his mouth is like hearing astrophysics from a Barbie Doll. Five minutes of finding the proper scanner, and five minutes of training and we were ready to rumble.

"Sign your lives away boys, and she's all yours." Handing the tablet back to Ken, we walked upstairs to Wilner's office still fighting over our new toy.

"How the hell does that thing work anyway?" Wilner tried looking at the screen.

"Well," Snake started, "The first thing you do is turn it on to seek, and then you call the number like so to lock in on the frequency." He picked up Wilner's ear piece and called the number out, and then hooked into the scanner. "Now the position of the receiver point will be superimposed over a digitally generated city map using satellite triangulation." Outside Wilner's office, at the very far end of the control room over the hustle and bustle of people and computers, a lone call rang out. We all looked at each other, then all looked to the dispatch center. Behind the glass, the dispatcher picked up his cell.

"Hello? Hello?" He looked at it oddly and then hung it up.

"No...fucking...way!" Wilner whispered. His jaw was on the floor with ours.

Beep! Snake looked at the scanner, "Third floor, our building, that corner. I love technology."

"You assholes spent some good money to look twenty feet away. Ellis go escort that dispatcher to me while I call up a full-time replacement. Oh, and tell medical to come up and give me his types. We have another donor coming in after debriefing."

Chapter 42

"All right gang, here's the situation! We've had a major breakthrough due to some honest hard work, a couple of assholes, and a lot of serious luck. At eleven tonight, we will do a complete raid of the target up on the board. You will muster with your assigned groups and brief on the objectives using the entire 3D generation our lab has graciously provided us on such short notice, and you will all be assigned areas of the building to clear and secure. Timing is the key to this being a total success, so listen well. May God bless you all tonight in this major offensive. Nobody is leaving the station, and all transmissions out are now effectively blocked."

Chapter 43

"All set to go guys and gals?" I was glad to be back at work with my team, I felt whole again, doing what I love.

"Ellis, remind me to kick your ass for getting me pulled from days off."

"Chomyn, think of the money you'll make on overtime and all the pretty clothes you can buy. All right, ten-second overview: on my mark we'll rally over to the top of the building at the same time as two other teams. From that point we will tie into the air exchange system and fill it full of smoke and Snake here does his thing with the computer system to register a fire on multiple floors. Deev Seven and Twenty-Nine will escort us in a top-down sweep of the building with our helmets and breathing apparatus mouthpieces engaged for filtered suit air, clearing stairwells looking for our assigned targets which will be downloaded onto your visor before we tie into the smoke and the computers. Our team will be playing in the penthouse, the entire uppermost floor. Once finished, all teams will rendezvous in the lobby of the building to sign in and then over to debriefing."

I pulled the microphone wire forward and engaged my helmet, "Deev Six a go."

"Deev Seven a go."

"Deev Twenty-Nine a go, on your mark Six."

The hair stood up on the back of my neck with excitement. I motioned everyone to engage their helmets. "Ok Six away, it's a go," and then Calahoo stood with her rifle moored and let her anchoring head fly. The rope whirred easily off of its holder at the front of Calahoo's gun. The first stage of the two-stage bullet had been designed to have the nose-section pierce whatever it was aimed at, brick, metal, or even meat. The second stage would pass through the hole the nose had made and expand into a nice little anchor on the other side, which we would then scurry across on.

"Seven away...and good."

"Twenty-Nine away, good."

I grabbed onto the rope checking that it was taught. I made damn sure Snake had finished securing to something sturdy on our end, then brought my legs up to meet the rope. Hand over fist with my feet sliding I crossed the to the target building fifty bloody storics above the street, hanging upside down. Finally across, I gratefully dropped – down to the gravel roof. I immediately stood and held the rope steady for the others as trained, while keeping a watch on the location. The other teams landed, and informed central that we were in process of tying into the air circulating system with smokers, which when ignited would smolder horrendously with layer after layer of smoke. Snake and Seven's tech finished tying into the building's junction box, gave the thumbs up and then flicked the switch on his geek box. We hit the smoke and counted while our targets were downloaded to us with mission specifics.

Alarms sounded from inside the building below our feet, and soon through the vents, we could hear total bedlam. "All right, everyone in, equipment engaged let's move!" We smashed open the top doors with the rams that were carried over and then Seven and Twenty-Nine ran in for their sweep. Throwing the rams aside, we went up into the penthouse which had been completely filled with blinding smoke. To the bare eye, you couldn't see your own hand held an arm's length away. I spread my team out after seeing the main room empty.

"Carrying west Ellis, all okay." Even though we were all trained for it, I know she was having a hard time relying solely on a computer-generated picture from the visor, and the alarms going off constantly made things even more disorienting.

"All okay? I'll carry on with east side to the south."

"Calahoo, come in." Nothing.

"Twenty-Nine in, I have something strange. There it is again."

"There what is again?" The voice of the Sergeant was confused. I knew something was wrong, I could feel the hair stand on the back of my neck. "It's just a small electric light, about the size of a pea with no image around it…"

I went cold, "Tell everyone to stand ready…" Instantly my helmet, display and all winked-out, like it blew a fuse or something. I hissed into the headset, "Deviance squads, code 312, repeat code 312! Outside surveillance needed on my floor!" Nothing back, now I was really concerned. I beat the side of my helmet thinking this would reset it, and then realized that the pillows had been slowly deflating. The helmet was completely shut down! I ripped my helmet off and threw it aside, we were in deep shit!

I pulled my scrambler up and shot twice. I heard a thump on the floor and flipped out. "Fuck me! Everyone stay low and look high we have insulated suits and mouthpieces everywhere on the floor. The floor we are dealing with is hot! Shoot twice with a scrambler!" I just hoped they could hear me over the fire alarms that still wailed. I quickly placed the mouthpiece back on to cover my mouth and started to crawl along the side of the wall. This would be both my guide and my cover. I just hoped I would bump into a landmark so I could get my wits and try to affect some change here in a hurry.

Snake, I just about killed him. I realized it was him after a few punches were exchanged. "Get the hell out of here and have the geeks pull this smoke out of here, all of the units are in deep shit, we were set up!"

"What about the girls?"

"Don't worry about them, I'll find them! We are sitting ducks in here without the helmets!"

"Roger that Sarge, I'll see you in a bit." About this time, the sprinkler system kicked in to create more confusion, but also helped thin out some of the smoke.

Crawling along the wall still I came upon Chomyn with her helmet off too, sobbing. "Roger, I can't find Calahoo!"

"Leave her and get the hell out of here back the way I came." Chomyn started to crawl along the wall on her belly back the way I had come, clawing more and more frantically as the thought of being totally vulnerable chased her along.

Suddenly, through the clearing smoke she saw the outline of a figure. She rushed for the body, she needed to help Calahoo. Just as she reached out to turn the body over and look, it rolled over. "Nighty-night." Before a breath of a scream came out of her mouth, Chomyn was hit hard and fast, and was out.

Chapter 44

I continued frantically crawling along the wall looking for Calahoo. I had to get to get my team out. Through the thinning smoke I saw a figure on the ground next to the wall I was approaching. My heart sank, it was Calahoo. I raced to her and picked her shoulders off the ground, but her head fell almost all the way back to the middle of her shoulders. Her throat had been cut to the spine, and my head started spinning, I was sick and couldn't compose myself. Out of the corner of my eye, I saw a silhouette of a figure run out of the room. I lost all proper thought and I gently set Calahoo down. I was after blood now.

Chapter 45

Odd, the figure was running up the stairwell to the top of the building from the penthouse. Forcing myself to calm down and be logical not reactive while winding my way up the stairs, and then burst through the door. I raced to get to the top level, looking all the time for an ambush as I careened over the railing to look up at the landing above me every so often. Finally through the door at the top…totally exposed! Anger had taken over and put me in this position. All I could focus on was the figure I was chasing on one of our wires trying to get across to another building and safety. I wanted him off so I could beat him to a pulp. I let a burst of my scrambler off as I screamed! I hit the target and he fell from the wire to the roof below. Without warning, I was knocked ass over tits. My head was spinning, and the red curtain blurring my vision slowly faded.

"Please get up, Mr. Ellis." The kick to my ribs I got lifted me up to my hands and knees into the fetal position at least, but it certainly didn't help me get my wits about me any quicker. I rolled onto my back sucking air like some pitiful animal dying. Dad always said blind-siding someone is the best thing to do to get the upper hand.

"All right all right, back off and let the man get his wits about him."

I know that voice, "Eihner, you sonofabich!" Rasping, but I was just finally starting to get some air into my lungs. I rolled back onto my ass holding my ribs, so at least I could see what was coming from a defensive position, spinning on my ass with my knees up.

"Mr. Ellis welcome to my world. I'd like to thank you for the inconvenience you have made for my family here, but don't despair. I have all I need here in my hand." He held up a bio-chip the size of a thumbnail hanging from a ball chain around his neck. He gingerly tucked it back into his shirt and patted it as if it were a dear friend. "Now all I need is a little lift off of the roof with a few of my favorite people I have here, and I can be up and running within a week at a new, hopefully idiot-proof building." Pointing at me.

I slowly pulled myself to my feet with as little show of effort as possible. The moaning and groaning obviously ruined the façade.

"Don't try to be the hero for our sakes, Mr. Ellis." He was laughing now. "I hear the helicopter coming for us." A few short claps from Jonas, "Everyone, places please." About ten suited staff circled Eihner. "Alle my dear, please cut all the wires so we have no other visitors to ruin this lovely function."

I turned to see the figure I had shot pull itself up from the gravel and brushed off, and removed her balaclava. Looking at me, and then with big smile revealed an insulator with a red blinking light then reached into the back of her mouth and with obvious discomfort pulled the bloody thing out and threw it to the ground, spitting. She wiped her mouth with her forearm, scowling at me. In one fluid motion she turned and shot all three wires loose from their moorings.

"Alle, Eihner tried to kill you. Why are you doing this?"

The whine of the helicopter's cell motor was growing louder yet. Eihner's support staff closed into a tighter circle around him, and then readied for the now visible military class helicopter that would take next to an act of God to bring down. How deep-seated were these people?

"Roger, you still don't get it do you? They were there for me when no one else was. You need to get that through your head. They helped me, they educated me, they trained me, they trusted me, they…loved me." She looked at Eihner with puppy dog affection, and he just smiled back, gloating. "Why would you think they would want me dead?" She came walking over to me and stood above me where I sat. I tried standing to look her in the eyes, but I saw some really ugly guns waving me to sit.

Quietly so only the two of us could hear. "But what about the messages Alle? Is my sister in there somewhere? I need to know." I was totally oblivious to the helicopter cresting the building and setting – down on the landing pad a couple of hundred feet away from us.

"Yes, I know," she said quietly, bowing her head but still facing me. She discreetly pulled a ball chain through the shirt of her heat insulating suit to reveal a chip identical to Eihner's! Fuck me, she went back to get the goods, she fooled all of us!

"Alle my dear, it's time to go." Eihner called. She turned to find a vintage combustion gun leveled no more than fifty feet away from her chest. "I'm sorry my dear." The flash of the gun was the only thing I saw, the chopper drowned out any other sound. Alle just stood there and took it, she always did. Her body fell lifeless to the deck of the building as I reached out and eased her down onto the roof. Hysterical, I jumped to her side and tried smoothing her hair, to take it back so she can live, to take one last look at her face. I had lost her AGAIN! I looked up at the chopper to see a sniper rifle being leveled at me, but I was frozen. I felt the spray of the gravel and looked up to see the sniper re-cocking the rifle. The dumbass missed the first shot as the chopper bucked and rolled in the swirling air currents it made as it broached the top of the building. I finally had to let go, again. Instinct won and I literally dropped Alle to run to the chopper's blind spot at the tail to the building's doorway only to find it welded shut. I could hear banging and thumping on the other side as the other Deev squads tried to come on the roof to help. The chopper swung around with its side door and sniper to me, I was trapped! I swear I saw my own reflection in the scope, then all of a sudden, the shooter's head vaporized. The headless corpse and his gun fell about a foot from the door, the length his anchor harness still holding him. I saw chaos and terror from within the chopper as a couple more people's heads vaporized on the spot. Eihner was in the copilot's seat screaming and motioning frantically telling the pilot to get the hell out of the area. The pilot and crew were safe from most small to medium arms as long as they had the shell or windows of the craft around them, but with the side door open they were vulnerable. I needed to take out the chopper. I took out a flashbang and concussion grenade from my kit. In the chaos, no one saw me come to within range of the chopper. I pulled the pins and landed them on target. From within the chopper came a beautiful phosphorous flash immediately followed a deafening bang. These were designed to confuse and concuss their victims to gain precious moments or hide the fact the granddaddy was there too! With the door almost closed, everyone in the chopper, regardless of the headgear they had on immediately had their brains and eardrums severely scrambled. The concussion went off, and even over the noise of the engines, I could hear the screams. The chopper lost total control. It pitched and darted and then clipped the edge of the building with its landing sled and careened violently. The pilot clearly wasn't conscious as the craft's main rotor clipped the raised portion of the roof access, almost opening wide enough to get a grown man through. The rotors came apart on contact, shooting broken knives everywhere. Like a toy, the chopper skipped over the roof, teetered on the edge as if were to stick there, then fell over the side to explode into a huge fire ball far below in the street. Over with, but wait…as I looked into the street below at the fiery mess, I noticed on the piece of fire escape ladders that the chopper hadn't ripped from the building on its way down, lay a twisted body on its back. From where I was, I could hear moaning and then a gurgling laugh.

"Eihner!!" This man had to be totally screwed in the head, he must have been delirious! He was still down there! I started working my way down two or three flights hanging onto support pins, pieces of metal, whatever, hurrying down to finish this prick off!

"Mr. Ellis…don't hurry down on my account. As you can see by my legs, I can't move them at all. But do give me some time to dispose of this." He pulled out his chip from beneath his shirt, and with great effort managed to snap its hard shell and circuitry in half, which he then painfully threw over the side of the building into the fire below.

I grabbed at anything I could to get down to him. I wanted to kill him with my bare hands and feel him pass!

"There we are, into the fire below and gone for the ages." He pulled himself sitting straight with his back against the building's brick wall, and then painfully straightened-out his crooked legs, screaming the entire time, so at least they appeared dignified.

I jumped down to the metal walkway with a thump, a few feet away from him.

"You see, Mr. Ellis, all of those bodies in the street and all of the damage? That was from the pursuit of one city. There is the Brotherhood in every city, at every level of everything. All of this mess for one ant in the hill? Hardly worth it hey?" Raising his eyebrows to me through his bloody face. "Lost poor little sis? Too bad, she served me well. I knew anyone who could kill her own father ought to be a worthwhile investment. You'll never win, you'll never see the end from your side, and it's impossible. I came very close," shaking his head at the loss.

"Roger, watch yourself!" It was Alle! She was alive, and looking down at me from the top of the building! Shit, she must have had one hell of a bulletproof vest on. "Oh and Joseph, look what I have here lover." He looked up and instantly the horror came over his face at the realization of the fact that she had the little black book to the Brotherhood on a chip as well hanging around her neck. Before I could even respond, I heard a click and Eihner lunged at me with a stainless-steel pick. Screaming in pain for his shattered legs, his fury overruled all. My scrambler went off in my hand instinctively, dropping Eihner where he sat, his mouth hanging open. No insulator, so he was in stasis.

"Roger, are you okay? Jesus Christ, just stay there, just sit and stay right there! We're coming down to you, you stupid shit! The last thing I need is for you to fall..." She just tapered off into a buzzing in my ear as I leaned against the wall and slid down to sit beside Eihner, to look at the big bad dead guy. With Alle and the chip, we had one hell of a head-start against the Brotherhood. We would be one team me and her.

"Hey shit bag, me and her will kick some serious ass, huh?" I smacked his crumpled body with the back of my hand, and the way he was laying his left arm fell back still loosely holding the pick. In the crook of his clavicle between his shoulder and neck, I saw a faint red flashing light under his skin. Total horror came over me! The bastard had an insulator hard-wired under his skin in the hollow behind his left clavicle! Before I could break free of my shock, Eihner lunged forward and planted the icy cold spike into my belly up into my heart.

"Yeah, you'll make one hell of a team," Eihner hissed, spit and blood coming off of his lips now.

I grabbed his hand so as not to let his pull the spike, which was now acting as a plug for my artery or whatever he hit in my chest. Slowly, I wrestled getting his hand loose and then folding itself back onto its wrist, destroying it and the four fingers I had in their joints. Screaming, Eihner tried pulling his other hand up to break free, but it was futile. I now had both of his hands in a lock. I leaned closed to his broken, blood-soaked face. "You know we won. Go fly now." He looked up at me dully, then when I pulled my legs forward from sitting and planted my leg onto his chest he understood. With all of my remaining strength, I pushed another piece of shit into the fire. Eyes wide, mouth in a soundless scream, he fell looking up at me the whole time. I heard a great metal thump as feet landed beside me on what was left of the fire escape.

"Rog shut up." She knelt down beside me to feel the spike where it went in. "Oh no." She trailed off.

"Why the hell are you saying oh no, I'm superhuman." I started slurring and feeling light headed. "Uh oh…"

"Rog you're going to be okay! We'll get you out of here, to a hospital, I can give you some of my blood. I'm your sister and it's easy…" Looking-up to the faces peering over the roof at us. "Are you fucking idiots trained to do something other than stare? Get a Medivac to the top of the roof immediately…" She kept going on and on, turning into inaudible buzzing. She kept screaming at the top of her lungs.

"Alle, hey come on." I put my hand on her arm, this brought her back to earth. "Alle, come on, it's pointless. I'm not stupid, I'm bleeding-out here." I tried standing.

"No, it's not so bad." She was pathetic with soothing, especially when she tried covering up the blood with her hands, trying to push it back in around the spike, somehow hoping it would help. Realizing it was pointless, she ended up straightening my collar, quietly sobbing. Frustrated, she dropped her hands to her side and slumped down beside me onto her ass against the wall, knees up with her head in her hands. She wiped her nose with the back of her glove, and then looked up to the sky wiping her tears away with her bloody hands. I am sorry I left you Roger, I never meant you anything by it, I just couldn't live it anymore…" Looking away. "So now what?"

"My little boy Gabriel, he's so beautiful. That is what this has been all about. He has an auntie now."

"And a father."

"Enough, you promise me you'll look after him with Adam and Emma like he's your own? Him and me are buddies. I won't get the chance to tell him to watch out for the world, to keep his head up…he's part of me…and you now. You promise me you'll teach him to be strong…and good, make sure he's a good man, to stand strong. I'm so sorry Alle, I was just a kid…I couldn't protect you; I couldn't do any better, it was what it was."

"I know, so was I Rog. Here I am now. I promise…the boy needs a good woman in his life for some balance, to learn to lift the lid, to share his feelings…" She looked at me, eyes full of tears, laughing quietly. "I can stand for both of us, I got it covered."

"It's all okay now, I see…" My family was complete.

"What the hell are you talking about Rog…Rog oh no Rog don't do this to me. Someone, help…someone! Get your asses down here now!!!"

Chapter 46

Regardless of the rain and cold, I couldn't bring myself to leave my brother's grave. I was bathing in the glory of a fine, miserable day. I was so close to getting my brother back, all the years wasted being angry, gone. I felt a strong hand on my shoulder and turned to look up into the tender smiling face of Adam underneath the black umbrella.

"I think we should go now." I nodded and stood. "A little boy is waiting in the car for his auntie."

I stood, and he took my arm in his to take me home.